The Rising Son
Harborview Immortals #2
By
C.L. Ingro

Table of Contents

Xan knew that he was dreaming. He had been here before. But this version of Steven's basement was a blood-drenched facsimile of its real world counterpart. There was an outrageous amount of it splattered across the grey brick walls and concrete floor. The smell of it filled his nose, thick and pungent. A closer look revealed grisly chunks of something (or someone) contributing to the gore.

As awful as the scenery was, that wasn't the truly frightening part of this burgeoning nightmare. The truly frightening part was the beast in the black suit that descended the basement steps. A left hand, pale and laced with black veins, clutched the railing for support while footfalls echoed thunderously throughout the room.

"I have a gift for you," the monster growled from the bottom of the stairs. It turned toward Xan and waited for a reply, its face concealed by a darkness that did not extend to the rest of the basement.

Xan's lips moved, but no sound came forth. He stood frozen, rooted in place, and terror enveloped him like a shroud. Lucidity didn't come often for him during slumber, and it couldn't have picked a worse time than now. *This is just a dream*, he reminded himself, though the thought held no comfort in the face of imminent demise.

Black Oxfords shuffled across the floor. The monster stepped into view.

Just a dream just a dream just a dream.

Jet black eyes gazed hungrily at the young man. Pasty skin cracked and split beneath a scraggly beard as an appalling smile revealed two rows of long, razor-sharp teeth. Gnarled fingers reached out, and Xan noticed a gold signet ring that was identical to the one Jacob had worn until recently.

He finally found his dream-voice as Vincenzo clamped down on his throat, gnashing and rending, cutting off his screams—

"Xan?"

Upon hearing Michael's voice, Xan opened his eyes. The sensation of fangs tearing into his neck waned as reality set in. He was back in his own basement now, safe in the arms of a vampire who meant him no harm.

"Are you okay?" Michael turned on the bedside lamp and placed a hand on Xan's heaving chest, frowning. "Your heart is racing."

"I'm all right," Xan said, covering his lover's hand with his own.

"Another bad dream?"

"Yeah."

Michael's frown deepened considerably. "That's the third one you've had this week."

Actually, it was the fourth one, but Xan didn't want to worry him further. He was convinced that the dreams would pass sooner or later. Surely they would. That they hadn't even started until almost one full month after his abduction had to count for something.

"I'm all right, Michael," he reiterated. "Everyone has bad dreams every now and then." When Michael opened his mouth to protest, Xan stopped him with a kiss. "I'm going to grab a shower. There's room in there for two if you want to join me."

He got up and stopped long enough to pet Aggie before heading into the bathroom, hoping that his offer would do the trick. Michael wasn't normally one to turn down a chance for mutual nudity.

After using the toilet and brushing his teeth, Xan started the shower. He thought about the dream while waiting for the water to warm up and was relieved to discover that it was already fading, as most dreams tended to do. It felt like a distant memory, something that happened days ago as opposed to minutes. All that was left were fragments, and those were much easier to deal with.

Following the incident with Vincenzo—who had foolishly believed that he could earn Dominic's forgiveness by turning his son into a vampire—Xan had contemplated the possibility and likelihood of some sort of fallout. He almost died in a gruesome way; it stood to reason that there would have been some emotional impact. But one week had passed, then two, then three. Life went on in Vincenzo's absence, and all was well until this past week.

The first nightmare, the one Michael didn't know about, happened on Monday. Vincenzo had him pinned to Steven's bloody basement wall and was moving in for the kill when Xan jolted awake with the smell of death and rot still fresh in his nostrils, positive that he had screamed out loud. When Tuesday came and went without any disruptions, he thought that the dream was a one-off. But Wednesday proved him wrong, as did Thursday and today, Friday. Now he was beginning to wonder how much longer he would have to endure them.

Steam billowed from the stall and filled the bathroom. Xan stripped off his shirt and shorts and stepped into the shower. As a spray of warm water washed over his tattooed body, he pushed aside the lingering mental image of black eyes and jagged teeth and, even more unsettling, the question of whether or not those traits had been passed down to his father and uncle.

There was a momentary rush of cool air as Michael entered the bathroom. Shortly after, he joined Xan in the shower. Xan stared at him, lips curving into a smile. Naked Michael was always a sure-fire way to forget his troubles.

"I'm well aware of your attempts at deflection," the vampire stated, his tone accusatory yet amused. "You did the same thing the other night when we were arguing over which *Diablo II* class was the best. One minute I was making my point, and the next, I had a head between my legs."

"Are you complaining about that?"

There was a devious gleam in Michael's eyes. "Not at all."

"You and your fucking Paladin," Xan scoffed.

"My fucking Paladin beats your Necromancer any day."

"In your dreams."

"Speaking of dreams..."

Xan groaned when he realized that he inadvertently brought the conversation right back to the topic he had hoped to avoid. He grabbed a bar of soap and lathered Michael's chest. "They're just dreams. They can't hurt me."

"Are you going to tell Dominic and Jacob about them?"

"Hell no. Even if I wanted to, there's nothing they can do about it. I'm just going to have to deal with them until they're done. Wasn't it the same for you?"

"What do you mean?"

"I mean how did you deal with all the shit Steven did to you?"

Michael traced a line of black ink down Xan's left arm, his expression thoughtful. "I met you."

He pulled Xan down for a kiss under the steady stream of the shower. Though the water was warm, Xan trembled all over. Michael's tongue usually had that effect on him.

"Turn around," Michael said after they parted.

Xan perked up at the command. "Now we're talking."

"Settle down, horndog." Michael snatched the soap from him. "I'm just washing your back."

"Oh, come on!"

"We have to be at your parents' house in an hour. It's bad enough that we were late last week. And then... that other stuff."

Xan grinned as he recalled that other stuff. After everyone else left, he and Michael had packed up the rest of his Transformers to take home and then fucked their brains out on his old bed. They had barely finished when Jacob suddenly came back. It was awkward.

"Fine," he said. "But you're going to make it up to me after work."

"How would that be different from any other morning?"

Xan ducked his head under the water to hide the goofy smile on his face. Goofy smiles made embarrassingly frequent appearances as of late thanks to the vampire currently rubbing and scrubbing his back. They had been together for a month now, which was a lifetime for someone who had never wanted a relationship until recently. Before Michael came along, the closest Xan had come to anything resembling a commitment was fucking the same guy more than once. Now? This. And this was good.

Nails raked along his sides, making him shudder. He raised his head and swept back drenched blond locks, then grabbed Michael's free hand and guided it downward.

"Xan..."

"What?" Xan queried innocently. "It needs to be washed, too."

He moaned when Michael wrapped his hand around him and squeezed, and again when he felt something slick and hard against the back of his left thigh.

"I'll be quick," he promised.

Michael gave up the fight. He turned Xan around by the cock and carefully got down on his knees. "You better."

HE WAS.

They walked into Dominic and Jacob's house at 7:55 p.m. Not only were they on time but they even had five minutes to spare. After saying their hellos, Xan tried to sit down on Becky, who took the hint and moved to a nearby loveseat with Demetrio so that the couple could sit together on the sofa along with Luca.

"You are such a shit," the Brit said as she crossed her legs and smoothed out her short red dress.

"I love you, too." Xan greedily attacked the tray of cured meats, olives, and cheeses on the coffee table. "What'd we miss?" he asked while stuffing his face.

"Becky was just regaling us with tales of her wild days in England," Jacob said. He then listed a number of well-known historical icons whom she had counted among her extensive list of former acquaintances.

"Wait a second." After running the numbers in his head, Michael looked at Becky. "You told me you were a hundred."

"Oh, boy," Demetrio murmured.

Michael continued, "It doesn't add up. If you were hanging out with some of those people, then that would make you at least—"

"*One hundred*," Becky warned.

"She's been one hundred years old since I was a kid," Xan whispered to Michael.

"And since Dominic and I have known her," Jacob added.

"Just nod your head and live to see another day," Luca advised.

Michael nodded frantically, ensuring his survival. Xan patted his thigh and joined the others in poking fun at him. He loved Becky dearly and went out of his way to show it by driving her crazy, but even he knew better than to bring up the question of her age. He much preferred that his body parts remained intact.

Dominic entered the room to announce that dinner was ready, and everyone went into the dining room. Tonight's entrée was cannelloni stuffed with veal and spinach, and the smell of it made Xan's mouth water. He and Luca eagerly dug in while the others passed around a decanter of blood.

"So, Domenico..." Demetrio filled his goblet and beamed at his twin. "How much do you love me?"

Dominic leveled a green-eyed glare at the vampire. "Not nearly enough to justify whatever you're about to ask me."

"Let Niccolo Alessandrini sing at the Rising Sun."

"No."

"Why not?"

Accepting the decanter from Becky, Dominic let out an exasperated sigh. "Demetrio, you are not going to use my club for your sexual agenda."

"Booty call," Jacob piped in.

Xan almost choked on a bite of cannelloni. "Don't start that again, Dad."

"Are you really going to sit there and act scandalized after last Friday?" Jacob asked with a raised brow.

"What happened last Friday?" Becky asked.

"Nothing," Xan and Michael responded in unison.

It was bad enough that Dominic, Luca, and Demetrio knew about the couple's Halloween exploits, or so Xan assumed by their amused countenances. When Becky pressed the issue, he told her to mind her business. She called him an arse. He called her a crone. She beaned him in the forehead with a green olive for his insolence. Xan grabbed a piece of garlic bread and prepared to attack, but Jacob put an end to the squabbling before the table erupted into a full-on food fight.

Never one to let food go to waste, Luca picked up the olive that had fallen onto the table and popped it into his mouth. "Nice shot."

"Thank you, Luca," Becky said.

Xan pouted at his former guardian. "Whose side are you on?"

"I'm neutral," the big man answered. "Pass the Parmesan."

A new round of bickering commenced until the sound of laughter cut through the din. Xan and the others turned to the source: Michael.

"I'm sorry. It's just that all of you crack me up. I'm not used to fun family gatherings. Or *any* family gatherings."

Jacob smiled kindly at the young vampire. "You better get used to them because you will always be welcome at ours."

"Absolutely," Dominic added.

"That's right." Demetrio reached across Becky's ample bosom and slapped Michael on the shoulder. "Anyone who defiles my nephew on a regular basis is family to me."

"Oh, my God," Xan mumbled, sinking down in his chair. But despite his embarrassment, he was overjoyed by his family's emphatic (and, in the case of Demetrio, inappropriate) acceptance. It was obvious that they all loved Michael.

Now if he could only decide if he felt the same way.

AFTER DINNER, XAN JOINED his fathers in their office while the others returned to the living room. He sympathized with Michael, who was practically dragged away by Becky and Demetrio, who would undoubtedly probe him about things that they didn't need to know. Laughing at the helpless vampire probably wasn't the best way to express that sympathy.

He sat down in front of the large mahogany desk and stretched out his long legs. There was a time when the tips of his shoes didn't come close to touching the bottom of the desk the way they did now. "Before you guys chew me out, I just want to say that whatever you've been told is probably a lie. Or, at best, an exaggeration."

"Is that so?" Dominic rested his elbows on the desk and steepled his fingers, his usual seriousness offset by the humor in his eyes. "Are you saying that all of the glowing reports we've received from Elliot about your new and improved work ethic aren't true?"

Xan was stunned. "Glowing reports? Getting laid has really improved his disposition."

Jacob lowered his head to hide his smile, but his quivering shoulders gave him away.

"What Elliot and Officer Goodridge do to each other is none of my concern," Dominic said. "Or yours."

True enough, but that hadn't stopped Xan from pressing Elliot for all the dirty details of their sex life ever since he and his parents had caught them fondling each other in the club's office. "I'll be sure to thank him for the kind words."

"Make no mistake, Xan," Jacob said. "You're a pain in his ass. But at least you're a competent pain."

Dominic nodded. "Before you came to us and requested more responsibility, he saw enough potential in you to suggest that you would be better suited for a job alongside him."

This was also news to Xan. He had gone out of his way to be a thorn in the vampire's side since day one; hearing that Elliot thought he was capable of more than pouring drinks was quite the shock.

"Elliot's praise makes us feel better about steering clear of the club while you settle into your new role," Dominic continued.

"We figured the last thing you wanted was to have us hovering over you," Jacob added. "This has also given us an opportunity to focus on the shelter, so everybody wins."

"Especially Tucker," Dominic muttered.

"How many times do I have to tell you that Tuck does not have a crush on me?" Jacob asked.

"Being a vampire is supposed to improve your vision, yet you can't see something so obvious. He practically humps your leg like a dog whenever he sees you."

Xan snorted at the crass—but accurate—assessment.

Dominic cleared his throat and focused his attention on Xan. "You've done well so far. You've learned how the club is managed, you're introducing Elliot to the joys of modern record-keeping—"

"Which he hates," Xan cut in.

Jacob shrugged. "He'll get used to it."

"And you're also learning how the blood trade works." Dominic tucked a lock of long black hair behind his ear. "How it works for *us*," he amended. "How we keep humans safe."

"Now it's time for your first test," Jacob said.

Xan wasn't sure he liked the sound of that. "What kind of test?"

"A vampire named Dionysios Katsaros will be visiting the club tonight," Dominic explained. "He wants to open an establishment in Chicago similar to the Rising Sun and will be spending the weekend in Harborview to get an idea of how things are done here."

"We met with him last night after he checked in at the Lamonte Hotel, and we've arranged weekend transportation for him," Jacob said. "Your job is to make him feel welcome at the club and show him the ropes."

"I hardly know the ropes myself," Xan argued. "Isn't this something Elliot should be doing?"

"Yes," Dominic said. "Unfortunately, his social skills leave much to be desired."

"Much," Jacob repeated grimly.

There was no debating that. Elliot rarely ventured from the office during club hours. With the exception of a pitifully small circle of acquaintances, he was not a people person.

Xan ran ringed fingers through his hair, which was no longer styled like the haphazard bird's nest (Jacob's words) it had been for so many years. "Okay, if the two of you think I'm up to the task."

"Do *you*?" Dominic asked.

"Sure," Xan replied, though in truth he wasn't sure just how sure he really was. But if his fathers trusted him with the job, then he wasn't about to let them down. "I'm on it."

"Thank you, Alexander," Dominic said, giving one of his rare and radiant smiles. "We're very proud of you."

"You've accomplished much over the past month. Don't think that we haven't noticed." Jacob approached the young man and ruffled his hair. "Now go rescue your man before Demetrio and Becky have him spilling all of your business."

"It's probably too late for that."

"Probably."

Xan stood up and regarded his fathers affectionately. There was a moment when his eyes met Dominic's, and the question he had pushed aside earlier surfaced in his mind for a second time. But he had no desire whatsoever to associate the monstrous face in his dreams with the one before him, and he banished the thought once again.

"I'll see you out there," he said before leaving the office to save Michael from two excessively nosy vampires and one neutral human.

DOMINIC STARED SOLEMNLY at the doorway through which Xan exited. The boy's heartbeat had spiked for a few seconds just now. Most likely it was the excitement of the job he had been assigned. That seemed like the most logical reason.

"You know what?" Jacob sat down in the chair vacated by Xan. "We have the best kid in the world."

"You're biased," Dominic observed wryly. "But so am I. And we do."

He got up and rounded the desk, then sat in the empty chair beside his lover. Jacob held out his left hand, and Dominic grasped it, his thumb slowly rubbing the gold band on the vampire's ring finger.

"Not bad for a couple of vampires who didn't know the first thing about babies."

Dominic grinned. "Not bad at all."

"I suppose we should get back out there before Xan accuses us of doing it on the desk." Jacob tilted his head, causing wavy brown locks to partially conceal his eyes. "Unless we *are* going to do it on the desk? I'm always up for that."

"We have company, Jacob."

"After everyone leaves?"

"Definitely."

"Nice."

They were halfway to the door when Jacob paused and looked at Dominic. "Do you think we should have told Xan that other thing?"

"About Dionysios?"

"Yeah."

Dominic considered the question and shook his head.

"Perhaps he'll find out soon enough."

WHILE XAN HAD ALWAYS been used to receiving a certain amount of attention at the Rising Sun due to being the owners' son, human, and easy, Michael was still learning to deal with the endless ogling and queries about his "miraculous" taming of Xan. It was at his insistence that they began entering the club through the back door. They still had to make their way through a crowd, and he still had to put up with the questions while tending the bar (along with the occasional phone number, much to Xan's chagrin), but it was *slightly* less invasive for the young vampire than using the main entrance where they were on full display the second they stepped out of Xan's car.

After parting ways, Xan watched him weave through the crowd on his way to the bar. He tried not to think about the way that heads turned when Michael walked past, or what body parts those appreciative glances were focused on.

"I still can't get over how well he cleans up."

With a heavy sigh, Xan acknowledged the vampire he had successfully avoided for the past week. "Stop staring at my boyfriend's ass, Paul."

Dark eyes glimmered mischievously. "You'll be happy to know that I still prefer yours."

Xan grunted and walked around the dance floor where bodies gyrated and swayed to a mesmerizing industrial beat. Paul was right on his heels. "You know you don't have to be here every night," he said as they stepped into the elevator that led to the lower—and much quieter—level. "You don't have to be here at all as long as Vincenzo gets his money."

An image of snarling lips and sharp teeth popped into his head, but he vanquished it before it could take hold. He pressed the button on the panel that would take them below, unaware of the way Paul studied him with a furrowed brow.

"Vincenzo is part owner of the Rising Sun," the vampire reminded him. "I will be here every night until he says otherwise. Your parents should be grateful that I'm not taking a more active role on his behalf."

Xan spun around, meaning to argue. But then Paul was right up on him, trapping him against the elevator wall. "What the hell are you doing?"

"What's wrong with you?" Paul placed a hand on Xan's chest, his fingers splayed over the silky black material of his shirt. "Why does Vincenzo's name make your heart beat faster? It never did before."

When Xan saw legitimate concern on Paul's face instead of the usual lust, he almost broke down and told him everything. But talking about the dreams meant thinking about them, and that was one thing he didn't want to do. That aside, he wasn't certain that he could trust Paul not to tell Vincenzo or anyone else what was happening. "It's nothing."

"Xan—"

The elevator doors opened. Elliot stared at the two of them, his eyes wide behind his thick-framed glasses. "Am I interrupting?"

"Nope." Xan stepped around Paul and stopped in front of Elliot. "Where are you going?"

"I'm meeting with Officer Goodridge to discuss the current state of security."

"Which is code for sneaking in a quickie with Brian."

"Shut up." Elliot stood aside so they could exit, his eyes narrowing in displeasure at Paul. "I'll be back shortly," he informed Xan.

"Got it."

The vampires on this level paid them no mind as they walked toward the club office. There were no advances made, no leering or sexual commentary. Most of them were close to or well into their thousands and had no interest in affairs of the flesh.

Paul followed Xan through the office door. "He still hates me, doesn't he?"

"Who, Elliot?" Xan saw no reason to sugarcoat the truth. "Yeah. It's not really *you*, though. Just who you represent."

"I can't do anything about that."

"No, you can't."

Xan took a seat behind the desk and scowled at the towering stacks of documentation that tracked decades of blood, alcohol, and vampires. Last week, he initiated the daunting task of transferring the information into a computer program and had vigorously worked his way through the year 2000. Only fourteen more years to go until he was all caught up.

He tensed as Paul stepped behind him. The smell of the vampire's cologne brought to mind a not too distant memory of an introductory blowjob in his private bathroom. Xan's heart may have belonged to another, but his body recalled the experience fondly.

"Are you going to answer my question?" Paul reached over him and grabbed a single sheet of paper detailing the specifics of a night back in January 2001. "About Vincenzo?"

"No."

The vampire dropped the paper on the desk and sat down next to Xan. "Your prerogative. What about my other question?"

"What question is that?" Xan asked, feigning ignorance.

"The question you've been avoiding for the past month. Are you still attracted to me?"

Xan kept his eyes trained on the desk, although he was very much aware of the well-dressed and inviting body seated beside him. "I'm in a relationship now, Paul. What's the point of asking?"

"I'm curious. Humor an old man."

"You're hardly old." Xan toyed with the sleeve that concealed the stake he had used to stab Vincenzo in the back. Taking a deep breath, he faced the gorgeous vampire. "Of course I'm still attracted to you," he admitted. "Inanimate objects would be attracted to you. But it doesn't matter. Now get out of here and let me do my job."

Smiling slyly, Paul stood up and walked around the desk, his fingers tracing the many platinum hoops that ran up the length of Xan's right ear as he moved past him. "It matters to me," he said as he walked toward the door. "I'll see you later."

After Paul left the office, Xan buried his face in his hands. The entire right side of his face was still tingling from the vampire's touch.

"Are you all right?" Elliot asked sometime later.

Xan peered at him through his fingers. He hadn't even heard him enter the room.

"Yeah," he said, sitting up. "How's Brian? I don't get to talk to him too much now that I park in the back."

"He's fine."

"Did he get you off?"

Elliot sat down. "I'm not about to dignify that with an answer."

"That's answer enough," Xan responded with a smirk. "Have a look."

He nudged Elliot's arm out of the way and reached for the mouse. After a few clicks, he brought up a spreadsheet dated June 1992, the month and year of his birth.

"There you go," he said, tapping the screen. "An entire month of chicken scratch on one easy-to-read page."

"My handwriting is not chicken scratch." Elliot checked out the spreadsheet, his frown gradually fading away. "That is somewhat convenient," he begrudgingly conceded.

"Thank you, Elliot," Xan said, smiling proudly.

The vampire was surprised by the use of his actual name. "You called me Elliot for a change. There's hope for you yet."

Xan couldn't have that. "So who tops? You or Brian?"

"I spoke too soon." Elliot got up and went into the vault, mumbling to himself.

"You sure did," Xan replied as he laughed merrily and went to work.

BECAUSE XAN WAS UNDER the assumption that his guest would announce himself to the two gigantic vampires who stood watch at the club's entrance so that a proper greeting could take place, he was caught off guard when Dionysios Katsaros casually strolled into the office by himself. And even more so by the vampire's appearance.

The guy was fucking *hot*. The kind of hot that almost made Paul look average. He had long brown hair that flowed over his shoulders, amber eyes, and naturally tanned skin. He looked to be about Xan's height, which put him around six feet two inches, and his lean, stylishly dressed frame didn't appear to have a single ounce of unnecessary fat.

"Wow." Even in his awe, Xan understood that this was not the most professional way to kick off a conversation and immediately corrected his error. "And by wow, I mean hello. Obviously."

"Obviously." The vampire smiled, and damned if doing so didn't illuminate his entire face. "You must be Xan Dawson," he said, approaching the desk with an outstretched hand.

Xan stood and accepted his hand. "And you're Dionysios Katsaros."

"Call me Denny."

"Denny it is. It's nice to meet you."

"You too." Denny released Xan's hand and glanced at Elliot, who had come out of the vault during Xan's initial drooling. "And you're Elliot Ledford?"

"I am," Elliot replied while pushing up his glasses. After a moment of hesitation, he walked over to Denny. After even more hesitation, he remembered that shaking hands was a thing that people did and executed three mechanical pumps of the arm before letting go and taking a step back. "Welcome to the Rising Sun."

Denny, who was clearly amused by Elliot's awkward formality, nodded graciously. "Thank you."

"Xan will give you a tour of the club and assist you in any way you desire while you're here. Please enjoy your stay." Elliot pushed up his glasses again, gave Xan a look that begged for help, and retreated to the safety and solitude of the vault.

"He doesn't get out much," Xan explained.

"I heard that," Elliot called out from the depths of the vault.

"I know."

Xan looked to Denny, who seemed to be enjoying the show. There was a gold coin hanging from a brown leather cord around his neck and Xan looked away so that it didn't appear as if he was staring at his chest. Even though he was. "I would have given you the grand tour before bringing you to the office if I had known you were here."

"That's okay. I wanted to have a look around by myself first."

"Before all the used car salesman talk?"

"I'm already sold on the concept," Denny said. "I just hope I can pull it off."

"Are there no places like this back in Chicago?" Xan wanted to know.

"Not quite like this. Most of the vampires back home don't have the same kind of respect for human life as the ones here in Harborview. I'd like to change that if I can."

Xan was impressed. While it was true that a large percentage of the vampire population in Harborview refrained from harming humans, he'd always had the feeling that such would not have been the case for many of them if not for fearing his fathers. On the other hand, Denny seemed genuinely interested in saving lives. All the money he stood to make from opening a club like the Rising Sun barely seemed to register to him.

"I have to tell you that all of this is pretty new to me," Xan confided. "I assume my parents told you that?"

"They did."

Wanting to make his folks proud, Xan attempted to atone for his first impression. "I'm sorry for the way I reacted when you walked in."

"Why? I wish *more* people did that."

Xan gaped at him for a beat before laughing. Did the guy have to be witty on top of all that sexiness? "I just expected someone who looked..."

"Older?"

"Yeah."

Denny wandered around the office, amber eyes taking everything in. "I'm seventy-two."

"You don't look a day over twenty-five."

"I was twenty-four when I was turned." The vampire stopped in front of a row of filing cabinets, his fingers sliding along the cool black metal. "Did Dominic and Jacob tell you anything else about me?"

Xan didn't know what to make of the question. "No, just your name. Is there anything else I should know?"

Denny looked at him curiously. "I don't know. Maybe."

Xan didn't know how to interpret that, either.

"Let's get out of here," Denny suggested suddenly. "Harborview's a pretty big city. Surely there's some place we can go besides McDonalds that's open all night."

"Um…"

"I'll have you back here before closing time," Denny swore. "We'll even stop by the bar on our way out so you can tell your boyfriend."

Xan didn't have to ask how Denny knew about Michael. He wondered if his dads had divulged that information during the course of regular conversation or mentioned it specifically to ensure that Xan's interaction with Denny remained business-only. His money was on the latter.

"Okay."

He stepped into the vault doorway and spotted Elliot shoving stacks of money from the previous night's take into a valise that would be given to Paul for delivery to Vincenzo. "You heard?"

"I heard. I don't need to tell you to behave yourself."

"No, but you kind of just did. See you." Xan beckoned Denny to follow him. "We'll take my car if you don't mind."

"We'll do whatever you want."

Xan thought it best not to reply to such a tempting statement.

MICHAEL COULDN'T BELIEVE how much his life had changed in such a short period of time. Two months ago, he was a student at Mercymore College working diligently toward a bright and boring future in Chemical Engineering. His father was an asshole, freedom was an unattainable dream, and vampires didn't exist. For all he knew, Hideaki Fukuhara was still an asshole. But he had finally achieved the freedom he craved his entire life because of becoming the thing he hadn't believed in. Fate had a marvelous sense of humor.

He had come a long way since the first night he arrived at the Rising Sun as a starving and desperate fledgling who was willing to part with his dignity for a glass of blood. Now he was on the other side of the bar, right where Xan had stood while serving him for the first time. He was no longer fleeing from the crazed vampire who turned and tortured him, or contemplating if dumpsters would protect him from the sunlight. Thanks to Xan and his parents, he was making his own way in the world, on his own terms.

"Hey, newbie," Ginger said, cutting off his reflection. "You've been wiping that same spot for five minutes."

Michael tossed the towel on the back counter. "How long are you going to call me that?"

"Until I'm done."

"Great."

Ginger rocked her head to the music, her red hair swaying to and fro. "It's a hell of a lot nicer than most of the names I called your partner," she said before shuffling off to dispense refills where they were needed.

Partner. Michael repeated the word in his head. He liked it better than boyfriend. It felt deeper. Permanent.

He was still ruminating when Xan stepped up to the bar.

"Hey, sexy thing."

Michael could feel interested gazes all around, but his attention was focused solely on the man before him. *His* man. "What's up? Do you want a drink?"

"No, thanks. I just wanted to let you know that I'm taking off for about an hour or two." Using his head, Xan motioned over his shoulder. "That vampire I told you about, he wants to talk somewhere less crowded."

Michael looked past Xan and tried not to gawk. "Wow."

"Yeah, that's what I said. He is not unattractive."

"Just promise me you'll keep your clothes on."

Xan reached out and curled his fingers through Michael's. A simple gesture that made his dead heart soar. "You can take them off yourself when we get home."

"I'm going to hold you to that."

"You'll be holding more than that."

"Stop it." Michael was glad that vampires couldn't blush. "Have fun."

He watched as Xan walked away (after giving Ginger a wave and a middle finger) and tracked them until they were no longer visible in the crowd. Anyone else might have been a little apprehensive about seeing their other half leave with someone that good-looking, especially if that other half had a reputation for getting around. But Michael trusted Xan, and he wasn't the least bit bothered by the scores of vampires who couldn't seem to stay away from him.

Except for one.

"What would you like, Paul?" he asked the vampire who had taken a seat at the bar.

"Xan, naked in my bed," Paul answered with a sneer. "But I'll settle for a Ghisa."

Michael went to get Paul's beer while indulging in fantasies of smashing the bottle right across his smug mouth. Having to deal with him was the one downside to an otherwise perfect job, but Michael would suck it up just like he did every other night that Paul entertained himself at his expense.

"Thank you," Paul said when Michael returned with his drink. He slid a fifty dollar bill across the bar top and grabbed the bottle. "Who was that with Xan?"

"None of your business." Michael snatched up the bill. "I'll be back with your change."

"Keep it. I'm not done drinking." Paul sipped his beer. "You don't care that he just up and disappears with handsome strangers?"

"Not as much as you, apparently."

"I'm just a concerned bystander."

"Sure you are. Look…" Michael planted his hands on top of the bar. So much for sucking it up tonight. "I'm sorry that Vincenzo left you behind and that I ruined whatever you had going on with Xan before he met me, but I would really appreciate it if you stopped taking your frustrations out on me."

"You're cute when you're angry."

"Fuck you, Paul."

"Is that an invitation?" Dark eyes deliberately looked Michael up and down. "I don't mind threesomes."

Michael moved away from the vampire's lascivious smile before he followed through with his urge to assault him with a bottle. Luckily, Ginger had gone on break after Xan's parting middle finger salute and was now most likely somewhere in the back, chatting away on the phone with Becky. He didn't want her to see his near nightly ordeals with Paul and tell Xan about them, and now that he thought about it, Paul must have felt the same way because he never seemed to strike until she was out of the picture. The prick.

After taking care of a few more thirsty clubbers and double-checking the blood levels (it was a busy night, but there was enough left to last until close), he wiped down the counter again. While doing so, he looked out on the dance floor. Bodies were everywhere, moving to the beat of the music. *Fuck*-music, as Jacob had called it one Friday night at dinner, which Michael found hilariously accurate. As his gaze moved over the crowd, he spotted one vampire in the middle of it all standing there. Just standing.

And looking right at him.

Michael stopped, his hand mid-swipe. He didn't mind so much being stared at; he'd grown quite accustomed to it since his relationship with Xan became public knowledge. But it was the *way* that the vampire was staring at him, like he knew exactly who Michael was, and not just because of Xan. This, too, might not have bothered Michael... if the vampire had been anything other than Japanese. Even with Harborview's diverse vampire population—if the wide variety of races and nationalities among the club attendees was any indication—Michael only knew of one Japanese vampire in the area, and all he had to do to find him was look in a mirror. Seeing another one, especially one who seemed to recognize him, was most unexpected.

The vampire kept on looking, unfazed by the chaos that surrounded him. He was physically older than Michael, by at least a decade, though that was no reliable indicator of vampire age. His hair was long, but Michael couldn't tell just how long from where he stood.

His first thought was that his father had somehow located him, but that was impossible. Dominic and Jacob had pulled many strings to safeguard his new existence from the human world. Even in the highly unlikely event that Hideaki contacted the authorities to report his son missing, Michael would not be found.

Maybe the answer wasn't that complicated. Maybe this vampire was just happy to see a face like his.

"Here." Ginger handed him a shot glass filled with red liquid. "Have a Red Headed Slut."

It was too easy. Michael opened his mouth—

"Careful," Ginger warned.

—and closed it with a snap.

"Cheers." She tapped her glass to his.

Michael downed his shot in one gulp. It wasn't half-bad.

"Next time we'll have a Minty Asshole," Ginger told him. "I bet you'd like that."

Michael grinned as she made her way along the bar and accosted the other bartenders. Talking to Becky always made her giddy, and it was pretty damned adorable.

Remembering the stranger, Michael turned toward the dance floor to find him. He scanned the entire room to no avail.

The mysterious vampire was gone.

"Huh."

He resumed taking and filling drink orders. After a while, he became so distracted that the vampire slipped from his mind completely.

XAN CHOSE JENKINS, a run-of-the-mill chain restaurant that was popular in Pennsylvania. There were three of them in Harborview alone. He led Denny to a booth in the far corner near the kitchen door, where they spent an hour talking about the Rising Sun and how the success of that club could be duplicated in Chicago. Denny didn't think that darkwave and techno would work for his neck of the woods, but his biggest concern was having enough blood to meet the demand. Dominic and Jacob had the Dawson House, their homeless shelter/blood farm. Denny wasn't so fortunate.

After all of that, he grilled Xan about more personal matters.

"So Elliot and Mr. Hot Cop are a couple," he said, mystified. "The same Elliot who couldn't leave the room fast enough when I was there?"

"If you hang around him long enough, he loosens up," Xan responded. "More or less."

"I'm intrigued." The vampire sipped black coffee before continuing. "Okay, let me see if I remember this next thing. The redhead, Ginger, is dating your best friend."

"Becky."

"And she has kids. Vampire kids."

"Yeah. Three of them."

"Who would do that to a child?"

Xan took a drink of his Coke. "We don't know yet. I wouldn't want to be that vampire when my parents find out."

They fell silent as a server topped off their drinks. Xan tapped his foot to the Muzak version of a popular Billy Joel song while he waited.

"How long have you and Michael been together?" Denny asked after the server left.

"One month."

"That's not long."

"It is for me," Xan said. "Before Michael, I was pretty... open."

"Open-minded?"

"Open-legged."

Denny sputtered into his coffee. He grabbed a napkin and held it to his mouth, laughing into it. "If you find something you enjoy, you might as well do it often, right?"

"Exactly!"

It was at that moment when Xan looked past the flawless packaging and suspected that Denny just might make a good friend.

"I've pried into your business enough for one night." Denny propped an elbow on the table and rested his chin on the palm of his hand. "Now it's your turn. Ask me anything."

Xan fiddled with his straw, thinking. "Why did you ask if my parents told me anything else about you?"

The curious look was back. "Because your dads and I... we have something in common."

"You're all vampires?"

"No, not that. Well, I mean, yes, but not just that. Tell you what. Come to my hotel room tomorrow night before you go to the club."

If Xan had been single, he would have jumped at the opportunity without hesitation. But he wasn't single, and while he had every confidence that he wouldn't give in to any temptation, he also didn't think that he should purposely put himself into any situations where his resolve might be challenged. He was only human.

"My intentions are pure," Denny promised. "I'm just coming out of a relationship myself. Faithfulness is very important to me... even though she didn't feel the same way."

"She?"

"Sarah."

"Oh." Xan felt monumentally stupid. "I thought you were... Never mind. I was wrong."

Denny smiled knowingly and slapped a twenty dollar bill on the table. "No, you weren't. Take care of this while I go outside and have a cigarette."

"Just give me a minute and I'll come with you."

"You can't. I was given very clear instructions not to smoke around you."

Xan wanted to crawl under the table. "You've got to be kidding me."

"Are you surprised? These are the same vampires who banned smoking at their club just for you."

"I'm surprised that they don't strap an oxygen tank to my back. I wish they'd get it through their heads that they can't protect me from everything."

"I'm sure they already know that. It doesn't mean they're not going to try." Denny twirled a cigarette between his fingers. "They want you to live a long time and will do everything in their power to make sure that you do."

"I know."

"That's just it, Xan. You know, but you don't *see*."

"I don't see?" Xan blinked at his new friend. "What does that mean?"

Denny smiled warmly. And, Xan thought, a little sadly.

"Come to my room tomorrow night and I'll show you."

⁓ ❦ ⁓

LATER THE NEXT MORNING, Xan slid between the cool sheets of the basement bed he shared with Michael. It was smaller than the bed in his room, but a thousand times better than the old air mattress they had used until recently. Michael settled in beside him and reached for the remote. On the far wall, a large high definition television—also an improvement—came to life. Not to be left out, Aggie hopped onto the bed and curled up between the couple's legs. She busied herself by gnawing on their blanket-covered toes.

Xan snickered. It all felt so blissfully domestic.

"What's so funny?" Michael asked.

"Nothing." Xan rolled onto his side while his lover channel surfed. "How do you feel about driving my car to the club tomorrow?"

"How do you feel about your car being wrecked?"

"You're not that bad, Michael."

The vampire stopped at Cartoon Network and set the remote aside. "Where will you be?"

"I have to stop by the Lamonte first, so I was going to take my bike. Might as well, since I probably won't have many more chances to ride it before the snow comes." Xan scooted closer to Michael and wrapped an arm around his chest. "Do you still trust me?"

"Yes," Michael answered as fingers snaked under his shirt and tickled his skin. "Do you trust yourself?"

"I do. But..."

"But what?"

Xan bit his lip while trying to decide the best way to proceed.

"This past month has been so perfect. At first, I kept waiting to wake up one evening and freak out about what I'd gotten myself into, but it never happened. I love being with you. I love—"

And just like that, Xan had an answer to the question that had plagued him since the very beginning of their relationship. There were no bells or whistles or fireworks. Angels didn't burst into the room and sing "Hallelujah!" The realization of his love for Michael came about rather simply. And definitively.

It was all too much. He laughed so hard that Aggie stopped chewing on his foot to stare at him with ears perked up.

"Xan? Are you okay?"

"I'm way better than okay." Xan stroked the vampire's cheek. "I don't want to fuck this up, Michael. *Don't let me* fuck this up."

He gave him a long, body-tingling kiss. Aggie, having concluded that he hadn't gone crazy, jumped off the bed. She ran up the steps and out of the cracked open door of the basement to give them some privacy.

They parted sometime later, both of them shuddering and hard against each other. Xan dragged his nails along the tail of the dragon tattoo on Michael's upper left arm. Michael bumped their noses together, which was indescribably precious, and then rolled away from Xan and reached for the nightstand. After shoving aside his wallet, some spare change, and his house key, his fingers closed around a white paper napkin.

"This is for you," he said, handing it over.

Xan stared blankly at the napkin. "Just what I've always wanted."

"Look on the other side, jackass."

Xan turned the napkin over and found a sketch of a raven.

"I did it tonight while I was on break," Michael explained. "It's a little rough, but the final version will be better. I hope."

"It's just being permanently inked onto my body. No pressure."

"Dick." Michael shoved Xan in the chest before taking the napkin back and returning it to the nightstand. "Where are you going to have it tattooed?" he inquired.

"No clue. I'm running out of options." Xan pulled up his shirt and ran his hand down his chest along the maze of tribal tattoos that covered most of his skin. There was some untouched territory further down his torso, right above the tribal sun that was inked around his navel. "Somewhere around here maybe," he suggested, rubbing the area just above the sun. "What do you think?"

Swallowing hard, Michael placed his hand on the young man's hip, his thumb caressing smooth skin. "How about here?"

"That works, too."

Their eyes met. Xan yelped when Michael forced him onto his back and stretched out on top of him. Although he was physically bigger, Michael was much stronger and faster, and being dominated by the smaller vampire never failed to turn him on.

He brought his arms around Michael's neck, digits weaving through wayward black hair. A hand slipped into his shorts and curled possessively around his erection. Xan inhaled sharply and bucked his hips, pushing into Michael's fist.

"I'm not getting anything tattooed on *that*," he said breathlessly and yanked him down for another kiss.

FOUR HOURS LATER, XAN woke with a start. His fingers were digging into his pillow and his heart was pounding so hard that it felt like his whole body rocked with each beat. The dream was just like all the others, with Vincenzo's dreadful, murderous face the last thing he saw before his throat was torn open. Thankfully, Michael was out cold on his side of the bed.

Aggie nudged at Xan's leg with her nose and rested her head against him. In the faint light of the room, courtesy of the nightlight they kept plugged in on the far wall near the stairs, he could see her blinking at him with those big brown eyes. Michael once told him of a conversation he'd had with Becky about the dog's eerie way of understanding, and that appeared to be the case now with the way she was behaving.

After giving her a scratch between the ears, he got up and crept toward the bathroom. When he got there, he went to the sink and scrubbed at his face with cold water as if doing so could wash away the remnants of the dream. The more he scrubbed, the more the fear he had felt in his sleep gave way to agitation. He thought that after everything that happened that morning, what with finally coming to terms with his feelings for Michael and all the sex that followed, he would have been given a reprieve from the nightmares that were becoming commonplace. Unfortunately, his brain had other plans.

Xan dried his face and thought about the question Michael had asked him yesterday evening. He still believed that telling Dominic and Jacob about the dreams would solve nothing. If anything, it might have created even more problems for his parents, Dominic especially, and that was something he just wouldn't do.

He left the bathroom and grabbed his phone from the nightstand. Michael was still fast asleep, and Xan smiled at the sight of him wrapped up like a burrito with a tuft of hair poking from the top. He made his way up the stairs with Aggie faithfully following behind him, and he sat down on the living room sofa while she wandered through the kitchen and outside via the doggy door that had been installed for her two weeks ago. It was just past noon and he was exhausted, but sleep was the last thing on his mind.

His fingers slid over the phone's screen, scrolling through apps with no particular destination. He brought up his contact list and deleted the numbers of one-night-stands, from Joey to Greg to Danny-Denny-Donnie (who was actually David). He was just about to set the phone aside when he saw a name that gave him pause.

Xan pressed the call icon and raised the phone to his ear.

"Hey... I need to talk to you... I thought I might come over if you don't mind... When? How about right now?"

HALF AN HOUR LATER, after trading his shorts for jeans and leaving a note for Michael in case he woke up, Xan walked up to the door of a two-story cottage he had visited often as a child. As he flipped through the keys on his keychain to find the right one, the front door opened and saved him the trouble.

"Uh..." Xan stared at the man and woman in the doorway and then double-checked the house number to make sure he was at the correct place. "Hi?"

"Hello!" The man offered a smile and a hand. "I'm Tony, and this is my wife, Danielle. We live a few houses down the street."

Xan shook hands with the couple. He noticed a spot of dried blood on Danielle's neck and presumed that any telltale punctures from feeding had been healed before they were sent on their way. "I'm Xan."

"We've heard *all* about you," Danielle said. "It's nice to put a face to the name. And what a lovely face it is." She tugged on her husband's arm. "I've got to meet the girls at the Yacht Club at two. Bye, Xan! Have a nice day!"

Xan waved at the retreating couple and tried not to laugh when he saw that Tony was walking with some difficulty.

"Good grief, Uncle Demetrio."

He stepped into the house and went down to the basement. The scent of air freshener lingered in the air.

"It smells like flowers and sex down here," he said, scrunching his nose.

"A winning combination."

"Do you trust them not to tell anyone you're a vampire?"

"No. That's why they never remember that I am." Demetrio hugged him and led him over to a sitting area where a flat-screen television was on but muted. "What's going on?" he asked as he sat down in a chair and casually draped a leg over the arm. "Who do I need to kill? Please don't say Michael because I really like that kid."

Xan grinned. The vampire had a knack for making him do that, even when he didn't want to. "No, not Michael. Not anybody."

"Then what is it? Do you want to know where babies come from? Have you not had this talk with your parents?"

"Actually, you could tell me where vampires come from."

Demetrio's jovial countenance faltered. "It would have been easier to explain the babies. Am I going to need a drink for this?"

"Yeah, probably."

The vampire went over to the kitchenette. "Do you want anything?" he asked.

"I'll take a beer if you have one."

Demetrio poured himself a large glass of grappa and grabbed a Guinness out of the small fridge in the corner. Like most who knew his family, Xan was continually amazed by the differences between Demetrio and Dominic, and while he loved his father ever so much, it was during times like these when he also appreciated that Demetrio was nothing like him.

"Thanks," he said, accepting the bottle.

Demetrio sat back down and swigged his grappa. "So why the sudden interest?"

"I'm a history buff."

"Right. And I'm a virgin. Well, the short answer is... I have no idea."

"How do you not know? Isn't Vincenzo like the fourth oldest vampire alive?"

"Third oldest," Demetrio corrected. "He never had much to say about the vampire who turned him, and we've been around for so long that the truth has been lost to time. One of the more popular theories I've heard over the years is that we're descended from demons, but that depends on what you believe. If vampires exist, then who knows what the hell else is out there?"

"Demons..." It sounded like a stretch to Xan, but like Demetrio said, if vampires existed then anything was possible. And when it came to Vincenzo's true face, demonic was a pretty accurate description.

"Is this the reason you couldn't sleep? The pressing need to know the origin of the vampire race?"

Xan knew what he wanted to ask, but still hadn't determined the best way to do it. There was also the small matter of being afraid of the answer. But he had already come this far, and he couldn't back down now. "When a person becomes a vampire, they inherit their maker's power?"

"Yes."

"And you and Dominic... you both inherited Vincenzo's power, which makes the two of you pretty strong, right? I mean, if he's the third oldest vampire, then his blood isn't... diluted or whatever. Is that how it works?"

"Basically. The blood of an Ancient is far more potent than that of a normal vampire."

"Are the two of you... Can you... *shit*."

"We can't do that."

Xan smiled faintly. "I'm sorry."

"Don't be sorry. Just say what you want to say."

Rubbing at his forehead, Xan tried again. "Can you... transform... the way Vincenzo did?"

Demetrio sighed deeply and stared at his nephew. "Domenico was afraid that this was going to happen," he said quietly.

"He was?"

"After that night, he knew it wouldn't be long before you made the connection," Demetrio explained. "He never wanted you to know that side of him existed, but then Father had to go and fuck it up."

"Why didn't he want me to know?"

"Because fangs are one thing. Two pointy teeth, no big deal. But what we are when you get past the fangs and the flying and all the pretty stuff isn't pretty at all. He didn't want you to be scared of him, Xan. It would break his heart to know that you feared him in any way." Demetrio set the glass aside and leaned forward, one hand resting on the arm of Xan's chair, his eyes wide and full of worry. "The same goes for me. Please don't ever be scared of what I am underneath this remarkably gorgeous exterior."

Xan took the vampire by the hand. He hadn't known how he would feel when he found out the truth that, in his heart, he knew all along. Now that his suspicion was confirmed, the last thing he felt was fear.

"I know you would never hurt me, Uncle Demetrio," he said. "I could never be afraid of you. I shouldn't have said anything."

"You should have said something sooner instead of keeping this to yourself for the past month," Demetrio countered.

"I didn't even think about it until..."

"Until when?"

Xan let go of Demetrio's hand and rubbed the back of his neck. He drank deeply and placed the bottle beside Demetrio's glass.

"I've been having dreams about that night. Bad dreams."

He described the dreams in graphic detail, everything from the blood-covered walls in Steven's basement to Vincenzo's hideous visage bearing down on him. Although the dreams had always faded just after waking, telling his uncle about them renewed the horror in his mind. By the time he finished his description, he was shaking from head to toe.

"I thought I could just ride it out," he concluded, staring down at his lap. "I figured they had to stop someday. Now I'm not so sure." He raised his head to look at Demetrio, blue eyes pleading. "Don't tell Dominic and Dad about this. I don't want them to worry about me. I don't want you to worry about me, either."

"You're my nephew, Xan. Worrying comes with the territory." Demetrio got up and paced around the basement, grumbling in Italian. "I hate Father for doing this to you," he continued in English. "I hate him for a lot of reasons lately."

"Like what?"

"It doesn't matter." The vampire returned to the sitting area and stood near the sofa where Xan sat. "I have an idea about helping you deal with these dreams. It's crazy as hell, but it might be worth a shot."

"At this point, I'm willing to try anything."

Demetrio sat down on the arm of the sofa and propped his feet up on the black cushion. His eyes, as green as his twin's but far more expressive, studied Xan carefully. "What if you saw that face on someone you knew would never hurt you?"

"... Do you think it'll do any good?"

"It can't make things any worse, can it?"

"Probably not. Unless Vincenzo can kill me for real in my sleep or something."

"That's an Elm Street thing."

Xan rubbed at his eyes, which stung from lack of sleep. Would subjecting himself to a recreation of the monster from his nightmares really make a difference? It seemed like such a far-fetched plan.

So far-fetched that it might work. He had nothing else to lose, except for even more sleep.

"Let's do it."

Demetrio hopped to his feet. "I never thought I'd have a reason to do this again," he said, reaching for his grappa and chugging the rest. "It taps into a part of me that I don't like."

"If that's the case, then you don't have to do it."

"Yes, I do. It's for you." Demetrio put down the empty glass and took a deep breath. "Keep your eyes on the TV. Did you know that chick is a lesbian? I love lesbians. Almost as much as I love eunuchs."

Xan sat back, his hands gripping his knees. On the television screen, a popular comedienne was giving an opening monologue for her daytime talk show and pausing regularly for unheard laughter and applause. The basement, which was already cool to begin with, suddenly became cooler, as if a burst of November wind found its way into the room. Xan couldn't remember if he had felt the same coolness the night he almost died; there was so much going on at the time that the temperature was the least of his concerns.

"You can look now, if you're sure you want to." Demetrio's voice was muffled, like he was speaking with a mouthful of something.

Teeth, Xan thought, inching closer toward panic. *It's because of his teeth.*

This was it. He turned his head and looked at the nightmare that had come to life.

Gone were the green eyes Demetrio shared with Dominic. Now his eyes were pitch black from pupils to whites, and far more ominous than any fictional rendering. Skin that was already pale was even paler, save for a web of dark veins that stretched from the left side of his neck and up his face. Demetrio's mouth was closed, but Xan could see the protrusion of lips that hid what had become of his normal teeth. The vampire looked every bit the monster that Vincenzo did in his dreams.

But this wasn't Vincenzo. This was his uncle. There was a world of difference between the two.

Xan stood up and took a tentative step forward. Then another. This was the vampire who had taken him to countless movies as a child. Another step. Midnight ice cream runs. Another step. Given him his first sip of wine at ten and bought him his first Playgirl at seventeen, swearing him to secrecy in both instances lest Dominic murder him for corrupting his son. Another step. Loved him like a son and would have gladly died to protect him. He took one last step, putting himself directly in front of Demetrio.

"Your heart is beating so fast," Demetrio noted worriedly. "I'm scaring you."

"I'll be okay." Xan touched the vein-covered section of his uncle's face, carefully, as though it might burn (which was not possible given the iciness of Demetrio's skin). "Vincenzo didn't have that. The real Vincenzo, I mean. How come?"

"He was holding himself back."

"Are you?"

"Yes."

If this was holding back, Xan wasn't sure that he ever wanted to see the complete transformation. "Why did he look so much scarier in my dreams? How did I even know about all of the... veiny stuff?"

"Because he was in your mind. It's different from being influenced by a normal vampire. When a vampire like Father takes a human brain hostage..." Demetrio grimaced. "It could have been worse."

Fragments of conversation from that terrible night rose in Xan's mind. He had been so distracted by the aftereffects of his abduction that he had forgotten the reason it even happened in the first place. It was an act of atonement for hurting someone Dominic had once loved, long before he met Jacob. A human man.

"Did he do something worse to Giovanni?"

"Far worse."

"What did he do?"

"That isn't my story to tell. All right, I think we're done here."

The veins on Demetrio's face began to recede down his neck until they disappeared beneath his shirt. Xan was so fascinated by this that he did not see the precise moment when the vampire's eyes and teeth reverted to normal.

"I need more grappa," Demetrio announced. "And you need to get some sleep. You can take my bed. I'll crash on the couch."

"You want me to sleep here?"

"For a few hours, at least. I don't want you driving home as tired as you are now. Don't worry, I changed the sheets."

Xan was grateful for the offer, and he was so tired that he didn't even care that he would be lying in a bed where a threesome happened less than an hour before. "Thank you, Uncle Demetrio."

"Anytime, kiddo. Don't keep something like this to yourself again. Do you understand?"

"I won't."

Xan went over to the bed and kicked off his shoes. He flopped down on sheets that were crisp and cool and closed his eyes to better process everything that he had just witnessed. Over in the sitting area, Demetrio was on his phone, talking in hushed tones to Dominic and reassuring him that nothing was wrong. Of course his father would have felt the drastic change in his twin brother. Xan wouldn't have been shocked if Dominic had even gone so far as to have Luca do a drive-by to make sure the house was still in one piece.

Just as he was thinking that he wouldn't be able to fall asleep right away, he did, but not before he felt a comforter being tucked around him and a hand pressed briefly but lovingly on top of his head.

He did not dream.

WITH A FLICK OF A THUMBNAIL, Vincenzo Castigliane lit a match and touched it to the tip of the cigarette that was lodged between his smiling lips. He inhaled deeply, savoring the rush of smoke that polluted his dead lungs.

Even though his residual link to Xan's mind was now broken, he was in good spirits.

How long had it been since he last felt either of his sons let loose their inner darkness? One century? No, two. When his beloved Domenico had protected that despicable slave from his maker. Demetrio hadn't fully surrendered his control just now; the bloodlust was so great in their primal state that the boy would not have survived the experience.

He continued smoking and staring into space from his chair while Steven slept on the bed they were stuck sharing for one more day because the Buffalo vampire community was pitifully lacking when it came to daytime accommodations. His business there was finally done, and he was millions of dollars richer for it. Tonight they would head into New York City, where "Vincent Castle" would acquaint himself with a select group of human businessmen who were going to be overcome with an inexplicable and undeniable urge to give him access to their companies and their money. If things went well, he might even let Steven have a little fun with them seeing as how he had been so well-behaved the past few weeks. Not that he had much choice when the alternative was Vincenzo's unique and vicious style of punishment.

The ancient vampire finished his cigarette, lit another, and resumed contemplating more important things. His children hated him right now and that... hurt. He wasn't sure if he could ever earn Dominic's forgiveness—almost killing Xan certainly hadn't helped—but there was still a chance with Demetrio. Unlike Dominic, Demetrio hadn't severed their connection or completely abandoned his dark gift. Maybe he hadn't completely abandoned his father, either. Vincenzo could always hope.

And if hoping didn't work, there were other ways to get what he wanted.

LUCA RETURNED TO THE house twenty minutes after Dominic finished talking to Demetrio. Since the sun was still up, the big man went down to the basement to report what he saw when he drove by Demetrio's house at Dominic's request.

"I circled the block a few times," he began, sticking close to the stairs out of respect for the couple's private quarters. "Nothing looked out of the ordinary, except…"

"Except what?" Dominic asked.

"Xan's car was in the driveway."

"What?" Jacob spoke up, stunned. "Are you sure?"

"Unless Demetrio knows someone else who drives a grey '77 BMW."

After exchanging glances with Jacob, Dominic squeezed Luca's shoulder. "Thank you for doing this."

"Do you need anything else?"

"That's all for now."

After Luca went upstairs and closed the door, Dominic turned to face his partner, who was rightfully concerned.

"I'm calling Xan," Jacob said, heading for his side of the bed where his phone sat on the nightstand.

"Don't."

"Why not? And why the hell is your brother unleashing himself around our son anyway?"

Dominic moved over to the bed, peeling off his robe along the way. "Because of Vincenzo, if I had to guess."

Jacob sat down beside him, his expression slowly shifting from confusion to understanding. "Even when he's not here, he's causing trouble."

"He is rather good at that."

"I thought that Xan had gotten over what happened. Why wouldn't he say something to us about it?"

"We've spent all of these years protecting him," Dominic said. "I think he is attempting to do the same for us."

"You might be right," Jacob agreed. "Are we pretending not to know anything about this?"

"That would be best for now. We'll add it to the list of all the other things he's done that we've pretended not to know."

"Like the underage drinking, and the sex, and the sex, and the sex."

They got into bed, reminiscing about the many instances over the years when they ignored some of their son's more questionable actions. There were hours to go before sunset, but neither vampire was tired yet. So instead, Jacob stripped off his pajamas, turned out the lights, and suggested a pleasurable way to wear themselves out.

It worked.

AFTER LEAVING DEMETRIO'S house late that afternoon, Xan went home and found Michael wide awake and waiting for him. He told him everything that happened, from the dream that prompted him to seek his uncle's help, to the vampire's transformation, to his blessedly dream-free nap and cautious optimism that the worst was behind him. When evening rolled around, he handed over the key to his car along with a guarantee that Michael would not be stopped no matter how badly he drove; the cops in Harborview knew his BMW very well and always looked the other way whenever it bent or flat out broke the rules of the road.

Now, at half past eight, Xan walked into the lobby of the Lamonte Hotel with his helmet tucked under his arm. The art deco interior hadn't changed much over the years, giving the place a pleasantly dated feel. Six guests waited patiently for their turn at the lobby desk, but when the clerks spotted Xan at the end of the line, he was immediately given priority.

"I'll wait," he insisted, holding up his hand. "I don't mind."

One of the clerks, a tall hunk of man named Ramon, all but shooed away the guest he was speaking with and beckoned him forward. Xan didn't want to cut in front of the others, but Ramon wasn't letting up. He could feel their eyes on him, some agitated and some inquisitive, and he moved to the front of the line, apologizing every step of the way.

"I could have waited," he said when he reached the desk.

"Nonsense. Are you checking in?"

The last time Xan checked in—along with two online acquaintances for a weekend of drunken debauchery—Ramon had gone above and beyond to make sure his stay was satisfactory. *Way* above and beyond. It was a shame he couldn't have given him a five-star review for his cock, or for being the only man he had ever met who could pull off a pencil mustache and soul patch without looking obnoxious.

"Not this time. I'm just visiting."

"That's too bad. Who are you looking for?"

"Last name is Katsaros. He's a 'nighttime' guest."

"Understood."

After a brief search, Ramon found the information Xan requested. He wrote a room number and code on a slip of paper and slid it across the counter. "Let me know if you need anything else. I would be more than happy to stop by and give you a hand."

"I bet you would. Thanks, Ramon."

Xan grabbed the paper and nodded his appreciation. He went to the elevators and took the first empty one that was available, then punched in the code that would take him to the basement level. When the doors opened, he stepped out and went down the hallway toward Suite C, passing a pair of female vampires with assorted facial piercings along the way who were presumably headed to the Rising Sun.

When he reached the door to Denny's suite, he knocked and did a last second once-over to make sure that everything was in order. The door opened just as he was running his fingers through his hair, and Denny stood in the doorway, chuckling at his efforts.

"Stop primping. You look good."

"I was just making sure." Xan stepped inside and looked around. "Nice place."

Denny shut the door. "You've never stayed here before?"

"Not down here. Humans usually aren't allowed."

"Not even you? You seem to be the exception to all the rules."

"I've stayed on the other floors a few times." Xan smiled as he remembered the first time he stayed at the Lamonte. "I lost my virginity here."

This got Denny's attention. "You did?"

"Yep. Room 217, which was fitting because I *was* seventeen."

"Vampire?"

"Human."

"How was it?"

"Long overdue. It would have happened a year earlier, but my dads cockblocked me. Rightfully so, but sixteen-year-old Xan wasn't very understanding at first."

"You'll have to tell me all about it sometime." Denny directed him to a sofa. "Drink?"

"Water, please."

Denny poured two glasses of water and joined him on the sofa. He tapped on the helmet sitting on the cushion between them. "I bet they give you a hard time about this."

"Not as much as they used to," Xan replied. "I know they still hate it."

"Can you blame them?"

"No, but I can't not live my life because they're afraid I'll break a bone."

"I'm sure they're afraid of more than that." Denny took a sip of water. "One of the places back home where vampires mingle is a real shithole. They all are, but this one in particular. It doesn't even have a name. It's just this old, abandoned meat factory. I guess you could say that's all it is for vampires, too. Humans are allowed to enter, but some of them don't leave. Not alive, anyway."

Xan's grip on his glass increased while Denny spoke. He had heard about places like that before. Sometimes it was easy to forget just how fortunate he was that being the son of the two most powerful vampires in the area gave him certain privileges. Like living.

"About three years ago, I overheard a couple of guys talking about some club in Pennsylvania that was owned by the 'kings of the Northeast,'" Denny continued, tugging on the coin around his neck. "The brooding Italian and the scarred slave... and their human son. I was fascinated by the idea of two vampires raising a human child, considering what we are and all. It didn't occur to me until then that I wasn't the only one who saw humans as more than food. That's when I decided that I wanted to open a place like the Rising Sun. I contacted Dominic and Jacob and have been in communication with them ever since."

"Why did it take you so long to move forward with your own place?"

"I didn't have much pull back then. I had money, but that doesn't get you far when blood is the real currency. And I didn't know how many others felt the same way I did. I still don't know for sure, but what I *do* know is that I'm tired of seeing people die. So here I am. But that's not the only reason I came here."

"What's the other reason?" Xan asked.

"I wanted to meet you. I wasn't sure how I was going to get away with it at first, but Elliot's shitty social skills ended up working in my favor."

A line formed in Xan's brow. If Denny had known Dominic and Jacob for as long as he said—and he had no reason to think the vampire would lie about something that could be easily verified with a phone call—then it was only natural that he would want to meet them in person. But traveling to Harborview to meet him?

"Why me?" he demanded to know. "Am I the thing you have in common with my parents?" Xan's eyes widened. "Oh, man. We're not related or something like that, are we? Because if we are, I'm going to feel incredibly gross about some of the things I was thinking about you."

Denny's laughter filled the room. "We're not related, Xan," he said. "And I'm flattered. I'd be lying if I said I didn't have a few thoughts of my own."

Xan relaxed and breathed a sigh of relief. "Then why did you want to meet me?"

Before Denny could answer, the bedroom door opened. A young man in navy blue scrubs stepped out of the room and looked at the two of them. He didn't seem surprised to see Xan there.

"Excuse me for interrupting," he said to Denny. "The pain was bad tonight, so I gave him a double dose. He should have stayed in Chicago. Nine hours on an overnight train didn't do him any favors."

"*You* try telling him no." Denny stood up. "Thanks, Billy. Why don't you take a break? Say, thirty minutes?"

Billy excused himself and left.

"He who?" Xan asked.

"Alexios Katsaros." Denny's smile was the same as it was the night before. Warm, but with an undertone of sadness. "My father."

AS ALWAYS, SATURDAY night was the busiest night of the week at the Rising Sun. The dance floor was so packed that some vampires did their dancing in the air. Frivolous displays of power were discouraged, but Elliot turned a blind eye to it tonight (thanks in part to an extended "security meeting" behind the club with Brian that left him uncharacteristically cheerful). Meanwhile, Michael, Ginger, and the other bartenders busied themselves with pouring, mixing, and serving drinks for two hours straight before the demand finally dwindled.

"It's about damn time," Michael muttered while shoving a twenty dollar gift under the cash tray to keep it separate from the other money. He learned his lesson the first time after Elliot freaked out when the drawer showed an overage. Tipping wasn't normally done since everyone was paid so well, but there were instances when customers insisted, like with Paul, who did it just to be an asshole, and the two female vampires with assorted facial piercings who had left Michael the twenty. One of them had written *Lamonte D* across Andrew Jackson's forehead, but that, too, was an offer he refused. Even if he had been single—and straight—random sexual hookups just weren't his thing. He tried it once, and it got him killed.

"Elliot wants someone to take his boyfriend a beer," Ginger said, resting against the back counter beside the register. "I nominated you."

Michael welcomed the chance to get away from the crowd to visit Brian for a few minutes; the cop was pretty likable for someone who used to fuck Xan regularly. He grabbed a beer and popped off the top, then made the slow trek through the masses toward the front door. The skeevy old vampire who had felt him up the first night he came to the Rising Sun as a starving runaway saw him and instantly made himself scarce. He had avoided Michael like the plague after finding out he was involved with Xan, and that suited Michael just fine.

Along with Elliot's guards, there were a number of vampires in the parking lot, some gathering to escape the inside crowd and others taking a smoke break. Michael passed them all by and went to Brian's squad car, where he found him sitting behind the wheel and playing on his phone. He sympathized with the man, whose sole responsibility of keeping humans at bay seemed like the most boring job in the world since, as far as he knew or had heard, most of the living kept their distance from the secluded property. Then he remembered when Xan told him how much Brian was being paid to sit there and do next to nothing and didn't feel nearly as bad for him.

"For you," he said, handing him the bottle through the open window.

"Thanks, Michael. What do I owe you?"

"I'm pretty sure Elliot would fire me if I charged you."

"You're going out with his bosses' son. Firing you is the last thing he would do." Brian tossed his phone on the passenger seat. "How's that going, anyway? I don't get to talk to Xan these days as much as I used to."

Michael was tempted to point out that Brian and Xan had done very little talking when they were together, but he wasn't sure if the officer would appreciate his attempt at humor. "We're doing great. What about you and Elliot?"

Brian looked at him as he raised the beer to his lips, his eyes filled with a devilish glow. "I have no complaints."

"I didn't know him before the two of you got together, but everyone else seems to think he's happier now. A little less... um..."

"A little less Elliot?" Brian grinned. "He hasn't completely removed the stick from his ass yet, but he's getting there."

Michael leaned against the car door. "You guys make a good couple," he said while drumming his fingers on the side mirror. "I'm just sorry about how it happened."

"That wasn't your fault," Brian said firmly. "You had no way of knowing what your psycho maker was going to do to me. Besides, I know it looks like I don't do much, but my life is at risk every single night that I'm here. I understood that when I took the job."

Maybe so, but Michael still felt partially responsible for what Steven had done. He didn't think that he would ever get the image of Brian's mutilated body out of his head.

After a few more minutes of small talk, he said goodbye and started back. He got the distinct feeling of being watched, which was nothing new. As the feeling intensified, he looked around for the source and saw nothing out of the ordinary... until he turned to the left and saw a vampire standing between two parked cars.

It was the same vampire from last night. The one he had forgotten about.

Michael stopped walking and met the vampire's stare. His hair was much longer than he originally thought, and his black outfit was similar to a gakuran. Like Dominic, he was attractive in an elegant way. Just as Michael was debating if he should confront him, the decision was made when the stranger walked his way.

Up close, he saw that the vampire had about two inches on him. "Hi," he said uncertainly.

"Hello." The vampire's eyes scanned the parking lot and club. "It is very busy here tonight."

There was a softness in his voice that Michael might have found soothing under different circumstances. He didn't detect anything bad or potentially dangerous about the vampire, but Steven had also seemed like a swell guy at first and look how that turned out.

"Saturday nights are usually like this," he replied. "Are you going inside?"

"Not anymore."

Last night, Michael had suspected that his appearance wasn't random. Now he knew for sure. "Do you know who I am?"

The stranger did him one better. "Do *you* know who you are?"

The chill that shot up Michael's spine was unrelated to the weather. "Who are you?"

"I am Ichiro," the vampire answered. "I am... a friend."

Michael figured his next question was a long shot but he had to ask: "Did my father send you here?"

"He did not."

"Then how do you know me? I've never seen you before in my life."

"... You have not."

"What do you want with me?"

Just then, Brian yelled out to Michael from his car. Elliot had texted him, stating that Ginger was getting swamped at the bar. Michael checked his watch and cringed when he saw that what had felt like a five minute break was closer to twenty.

"I have to get back to work." There was much more he wanted to ask Ichiro, questions that would hopefully get him more than a cryptic answer, but now was not the time. "Are you sure you don't want to come in for a drink?" he asked, trying to entice the vampire into sticking around. "On the house."

"I must refuse." Ichiro bowed slightly. "Goodbye, Michael Fukuhara."

Michael slowly backed away. "Bye."

He turned around and headed back. He had a ton of questions and hardly any answers, but he also had a feeling that this was not the last time their paths would cross.

ICHIRO WAITED UNTIL Michael vanished through the club door before taking a phone out of his pocket and dialing a number.

"This is Ichiro. I found him."

XAN STOOD IN THE BEDROOM doorway of Denny's suite as the vampire rubbed lotion onto the thin, liver-spotted arm of his sleeping father. He moved with great care and ease, handling the limb like a fragile thing that could break at any second.

"He'll be ninety-seven in January," Denny quietly informed him while pouring more lotion onto his palm. He took the old man's hand into his own and massaged it. "He's got his good days, but not as many as before."

"What's wrong with him?" Xan asked.

"Cancer."

"What kind?"

"Take your pick. It's everywhere."

It all made sense to Xan now, the reason that Denny had wanted him there. He regarded the pitifully frail being in the bed, a human life drawing to a close. This was his future.

His eyes moved from the old man to Denny. The vampire exuded tremendous sorrow, trapped in time while the one he loved slipped away. This was his parents' future.

He had known the inevitable all along. Now he was seeing a preview of it.

Denny finished with his father's arms and tugged down the sleeves of his pajamas. He moved to the nightstand and checked the contents of a pill organizer before kissing the man on the forehead and leaving the room. After closing the door, he lifted his shirt to reveal a long vertical scar in the center of his otherwise perfect chest. "I was born with a heart defect. Doctors did their best, but it couldn't be fixed. They said it was just a matter of time before I died. It was a miracle that I made it to my twenties."

"Looks like you found a fix after all," Xan said.

Denny lowered his shirt. "My father had all the money in the world, but he couldn't buy my health. So he found an alternative. And I'm still here, just like he wanted."

"You became a vampire for him?"

"Don't get me wrong. I have no regrets about the choice I made. I like what I am. I *love* what I am. But yes, I did it for him."

"Why are you telling me this?" Xan asked. "You don't even know me."

"I know Dominic and Jacob. I know the fear they feel now... and the sadness they'll feel later." Denny gently touched the door. "My father's pain will end soon. My pain will last forever."

"Are you suggesting that I become a vampire?"

"I'm suggesting that you weigh your options."

"You think I haven't?"

"Have you? Have you *really*?"

Xan paced around the suite, his eyes focused on the floor and jaw clenched tightly. The conversation was steering toward a topic he hadn't confronted since the night he was abducted, and he wasn't sure how to proceed or that he even wanted to. He was well aware of his mortality; being surrounded by vampires was a constant reminder of it. However, Vincenzo's attack aside, the certainty of his passing had always seemed like a faraway concept, something he didn't need to think about for years and years to come. Until now.

"Do you know how my dads found me?" he asked.

"Yes, I do," Denny responded.

"If things had gone differently that night, I would have died." Xan leaned against the back of the sofa, folding his arms. "The way I see it, I've been living on borrowed time since I was born. Every day of my life is a gift. It's selfish of me to ask for more than I've already been given."

"That's one way to look at it."

"Is there another?"

Denny went over to the sofa and stood beside him. "Say a person gets a horrible disease, like cancer," he began, motioning at the bedroom door. "They go through the radiation and the chemo and all the other bullshit and miraculously go into remission. Years pass. Maybe even decades. Then one day, the cancer shows up again. Do they do everything they can to fight it or do they just say 'oh well, fuck it, I've been living on borrowed time all along' and wait to die?"

"That's different, Denny."

"How?" When Xan had no answer, the vampire continued, "You say that you would have died if things had gone differently the night your parents found you, and that's true. But it's not just you, Xan. At one point or another, almost every human being's life hinges on that one little thing that just happens to work out for them, even if they don't know it. Someone misses a plane that ends up crashing, or takes a left turn instead of a right and avoids an accident. Two vampires just happen to take a path that leads them to a baby in a dumpster. You see? It's all the same."

Xan pinched the bridge of his nose, taking in all of Denny's words. "Jesus, man. Couldn't you just want to have sex with me like everybody else?"

They shared a reluctant chuckle over the question. Afterwards, Denny clapped a hand on Xan's shoulder and gave it a reassuring squeeze. "Your life is none of my business, Xan. I know that. I just wanted you to see the other side of the coin. You are going to break a lot of hearts when you die. I barely know you myself, and I'm already going to miss you. Whatever you choose, do so without regret. My father told me that he regrets remaining human. I don't want the same thing to happen to you."

Again, Xan thought about the dying old man in the bedroom. That would be him one day, if he lived that long. Denny's suffering would become Dominic and Jacob's, and Demetrio's, and Becky's, and maybe even Elliot's. And, of course, Michael's. Did he really want to put all of them through the devastation of his aging and subsequent death because he felt undeserving of eternity? His refusal didn't seem so indisputable now that Denny had offered him an alternate viewpoint.

This was not to say that he didn't enjoy being human. Lack of longevity aside, Xan greatly treasured the freedom of having a mortal life. He didn't have to wait until sundown to do anything outside of his home (although he usually did, being a product of his environment), and he could eat whatever he wanted without repercussion, aside from the occasional bout of garlic-induced heartburn from eating Dominic's delicious Italian meals. Those things didn't seem like much compared to never getting sick or hurt or growing old, but he appreciated them nevertheless.

"Thank you for caring enough to be so nosy," he said.

"You're welcome. And for the record, I *do* want to have sex with you. But you have a boyfriend, and I make it a point never to sleep with people I'd like to be friends with."

"How's that working out for you?"

"I don't have many friends."

They shared another laugh, this one more heartfelt.

"Come on," Denny said, elbowing him in the side. "I think we could both use something stronger than water."

XAN DIDN'T KNOW ABOUT any future regrets, but right now he regretted the hell out of refusing to wear a jacket in a stubborn, last-ditch attempt to deny the arrival of winter weather. The temperature had dipped a good ten degrees during the hour or so he spent with Denny, and it was made even worse by riding a motorcycle. The one good thing about freezing his ass off as he maneuvered his way through the downtown streets of Harborview was that the cold air helped him to concentrate in a way that the two drinks he'd had with Denny couldn't.

He neared a street he knew all too well and switched on the right turn signal. Although he hadn't consciously planned to visit the Dawson House before heading to the club, his subconscious decided that was where he needed to go first. He pulled into the lot and parked next to Dominic's BMW. There was a Lexus on the other side of the car, and Xan smiled when he saw it. He was always pleased to see Tuck, who was often so busy getting felt up at the club that he rarely had time for anything more than a quick hello.

Xan removed his helmet and went to the building's private entrance. Since he didn't have a swipe card yet, he knocked and waited, suppressing a shudder as a gust of icy air blew around him.

"Hey there," Tuck said after opening the door. As usual, he was chomping on a piece of gum. "Why the hell aren't you wearing a jacket?"

"Because it's still officially fall, damn it."

"You know it's supposed to snow next week."

"I'll believe it when I see it."

Tuck led him downstairs to the collection area where an older-looking female vampire—Ruth, if Xan remembered correctly—was studiously prepping bags of blood and dry ice for delivery to private buyers. The room was hardly warm given the nature of the work being done there, but it was a vast improvement over being outside.

"I thought you only worked on Sundays," Xan said.

"I usually pick up an extra night here and there when the shelter's full. I don't mind helping out, and Ruth loves seeing more of me." Tuck moved over to the woman and placed an arm around her. "Don't you?" he cooed in her ear.

"Yes, Tucker, it's the highlight of my night," she replied sarcastically.

Xan left them to their work and walked down the long corridor where the shelter guests made their donations (before promptly being relieved of any memory of those donations by Tuck) until he came to an office on the far end. He knocked before opening the door, keeping his eyes averted in case his fathers were doing something perverted.

"Are you guys decent?"

"Hold on, we're naked!" Jacob yelled out.

"Seriously?"

The vampire laughed heartily. "Get in here."

Xan had half a mind to lecture him about scorching his brain, but to do so would have invited another comparison to Halloween, when Jacob came home and caught him with his zipper down. Instead, he stepped inside and glowered at his father while his other father read over a spreadsheet with a hint of a smile.

"What brings you by?" Jacob cocked his head when he noticed that Xan was missing a key article of clothing. "And why the hell aren't you wearing a jacket?"

Xan almost mentioned that Tuck had asked him the same thing, but he didn't want to spark another debate about the vampire's crush. "I just came from the Lamonte," he replied, hoping to divert Jacob's attention from his disregard for outerwear.

Dominic glanced up at him. "Were you visiting Dionysios?"

Xan had to presume that Dominic was well aware of Denny's preference for a nickname. He chalked it up to the vampire's odd aversion to shortened names, hence his insistence on calling Xan by his given name of Alexander and only referring to Becky as Rebecca. It was funny in an endearing sort of way since, according to Jacob, he was the one who came up with the nickname Xan in the first place.

"Yes."

"To discuss business?" Jacob asked skeptically.

"Mostly." Xan stared pointedly at his parents. "I also met his father. Well, he was asleep, but I saw him."

"That's probably the only time that poor man isn't in pain," Jacob commiserated.

"We weren't positive that there would be any cause for him to mention his father to you," Dominic stated. "I don't want you to think we withheld information from you for dubious reasons."

"I know you didn't." Xan elected not to tell them that Denny was the dubious one, at least where they were concerned. They probably wouldn't have been thrilled to learn that the vampire had taken it upon himself to broach the subject of Xan's humanity.

"How did your meeting go?" Jacob asked. "Do you think he'll be able to run a club like ours?"

Xan placed his helmet on the desk and sat on the edge of it since there wasn't an extra chair in the compact office. "I think so. He seems pretty gung-ho about it, but blood might be a problem. He doesn't have a Dawson House like we do."

"We're working on that," Dominic said.

"It won't be easy with our present distribution arrangements, but we'll figure something out for him," Jacob added.

"You guys should just open another shelter in Chicago," Xan suggested jokingly. "I like the idea of being a chain."

"We haven't ruled that out," Jacob told him.

"No shit?"

"It would be an ambitious endeavor," Dominic said. "From what Dionysios has told us, the vampires in that area don't seem too keen on preserving their food sources."

Xan smirked at Dominic's polite way of referring to cold-blooded murder. He picked up one of the sheets of paper off the desk and looked it over. There were four columns labeled TRS, TH, CCL, and P, and he worked out that they stood for the four-way split of blood distribution: the Rising Sun,

Tomah Hospital, Consolidated Clinical Laboratories, and private purchasers. Under each column was a list of various letter and number combinations like WMAB+1-1, BFO-3-6, and HMB+2-4 that indicated a donor's race or nationality, gender, and blood type, along with their present floor and room number. It was an easy yet effective way to keep track of what went where in a given week.

"I should get going. I hate leaving Elliot alone for too long."

"I'm sure he's heartbroken by your absence." Jacob grabbed a short black trench coat from the back of his chair. "Take this," he said, handing it to the young man. "I thought we were well past the point of having to dress you."

Xan put on the coat. He reached into the pockets and found a pair of black leather gloves to go along with it. "Thanks, Dad. What about you?"

"Dominic will make sure that I'm warm enough to make it home."

Xan tried to be disgusted but Jacob's laughter was too infectious for him to resist. He wondered if the vampire would ever laugh like that again after he died and mentally berated himself for ruining his own good mood with morbid speculations.

"I'll drop it off tomorrow." He tied the coat's belt and slid his hands into the gloves, then went around the desk and kissed them both on the cheek, something he hadn't done in a long time.

"What was that for?" Jacob asked, touching the spot that Xan kissed.

"Because I wanted to... and because I appreciate the fact that you didn't interrogate me about going to Uncle Demetrio's house earlier today."

"You knew that we knew?"

"Not for sure, but I figured."

Dominic studied Xan, curious and concerned. "Did he help you?"

"Yeah, he did. He helped a lot. So don't worry about me, okay?" Xan tugged on the vampire's long hair—another gesture of affection from his youth. He pondered for a bit and added, "You should let that Niccolo guy sing at the club. I can't think of a better way to thank him."

"I'm sure there are plenty of other ways to show gratitude that don't involve catering to his fetish," Dominic said. "But I will consider it for you."

Xan had gotten his way in life long enough to know a delayed yes when he heard it. As did Jacob, judging by the way he raised one index finger and made a circular motion around it with the other. Like he had room to talk about being wrapped around their son's finger.

"Thank you, Dominic."

"You're welcome, Alexander." Dominic turned to his partner. "And as for you, keep that up and you can warm yourself."

"You don't mean that," Jacob said, repeatedly poking the stone-faced vampire's cheek.

"I most certainly do."

Xan grabbed his helmet and waved at the duo while they continued their flirtatious bickering, his heart aching with love as it often did when he remembered that he had the best parents in the world. As he stepped out into the hallway, a single realization dominated his mind, one that made the so-called freedom of having unlimited access to sunlight and pasta seem drastically unimportant:

It could be like this forever.

HE MET UP WITH DENNY again at the club. To spare Elliot the agony of interaction, they kept to the main level. After showing Denny where the blood and booze were stored, they returned to the bar where Xan called forth his old bartending know-how and gave Denny a brief lesson in how to combine blood and alcohol. This also gave him a chance to properly introduce the vampire to Michael.

"He is goddamn adorable," Denny told him after Michael left them to serve others. "I can see why you settled down."

"Don't get any ideas."

"Too late."

Xan rolled his eyes at the winking vampire, who was working his way through a variety of mixed drinks that Michael had prepared for him. He caught Paul watching the two of them from the other side of the bar and discreetly shook his head in a silent warning for him to keep away and mind his own damn business.

"I'm still not crazy about the music," Denny said between sips of a Bloody Margarita. "Why don't you guys play some jazz or Rat Pack or something?"

"Because you can't do a standing dry hump to that stuff."

"I beg to differ. I once got someone off just by slow dancing to a Dean Martin song. It's one of my finer accomplishments in life."

They gathered up all of Denny's drinks and moved over to one of the tables closest to the dance floor. When they weren't discussing business or having a laugh over some of the more rhythmically-challenged patrons, Denny entertained himself by trying to guess which vampires Xan knew intimately. Given the depth of Xan's "knowledge," it wasn't that difficult to figure out.

"What about the guy at the bar?" he asked. "The one who's been eye-fucking you this whole time."

Xan didn't have to look to know who Denny was talking about. "That would be Paul. We weren't quite able to finish what we started."

"Why not?"

"I met Michael the same night."

Denny's eyes widened as he finished off a Cosmopolitan. "There's another story I can't wait to hear."

"I'll tell you all about it the next time you come to town if you tell me about your coin."

The vampire tugged on the coin around his neck. "How do you know there's anything to tell?"

"Just a guess."

"Good guess. You got it."

They continued talking and drinking until last call. Xan offered to walk Denny to the limo his parents had provided but the vampire declined since he wanted to smoke before leaving and didn't dare do it around Xan.

"Say goodbye to Elliot for me," Denny said. "And give me your phone number so I can send you dick pics sometime."

Xan laughed as he grabbed his phone. They swapped numbers and shook hands. After that, Denny looked to the bar and waved goodbye to Michael over the heads of departing vampires.

"We should all do something fun the next time I'm here. Nothing sexual. Unless—"

"Knock it off."

Denny grinned. "Tell your parents I'll be in touch after I get home."

"Will do."

After Denny left, Xan picked up all the empty glasses and brought them over to the bar. "Here you go."

"Gee, thanks," Michael mumbled.

"I was talking to Ginger."

"Fuck you very much," the redhead snapped.

Xan sat down while she cleared the mess. "Thank you, Red."

"Yeah, yeah, yeah."

"You should be nicer to her," Michael said after she walked away. "She's a working mother."

"I *was* being nice," Xan replied. "Do you want me to wait for you?"

"I assumed you would so you could make sure your baby got home safely."

"Why would I do that? I trust your driving."

Michael wasn't convinced. "Is that so? Tell me something."

"Anything."

"Did you check your car for damage when you got here?"

"I have to go to the bathroom."

"That's what I thought."

Xan chuckled at the vampire's surliness. He really did need to take a piss though, but not before grabbing Michael's hand and bringing it to his mouth for a kiss.

"It'll take more than that for me to forgive you."

Xan was about to suggest that Michael join him in the bathroom. Unfortunately, Ginger was back and giving them massive amounts of stink eye, so he had no choice but to go with Plan B.

"Hurry up and finish so I can try harder when we get home."

BUT WHEN THEY GOT HOME, their plans were put on hold after Xan almost tripped over a package that Luca had dropped off at some point during the night. *This came for you today*, the taped-on note said. *I'm sure you know porn is free on the Internet. I don't even like sex and I know that. L.*

However, the package didn't contain porn (this time). It was Xan's monthly order from Uptown Comics. He showed it to Michael, who responded with a broad smile.

"Meet you back here in ten?" Xan asked.

"Five," Michael countered.

After a quick peck on the lips, they hurried to their respective rooms to change clothes. Sex could wait. There were comics to be read.

Seven minutes later, they were stretched out on opposite ends of the living room sofa with a mutt dozing on top of their intertwined legs. Xan was reading the newest issue of *Manifest Destiny* while Michael tackled past issues of *Transmetropolitan* that Xan ordered for him after finding out he had never read it.

"For fuck's sake," Xan muttered, turning a page.

Michael peered at him over the top of his comic book. "What's wrong?"

"I've read so much manga that I catch myself reading the bubbles right to left. No wonder the story wasn't making any damn sense."

"Dork."

"Don't call me a dork, geek."

"Don't call me a geek, nerd."

Xan's playful kick woke up Aggie. After some firm back scratching, she was fast asleep again in no time.

The couple worked their way through the stack of comics as the night came to an end. Xan checked his phone. There was about an hour to go until they would have to retire to the basement for the day.

He made it halfway through an issue of *New Avengers* before his mind wandered back to the events of the night, and he closed the book and stared thoughtfully at the vampire across from him. Michael's brow was creased as his eyes moved over the page, concentrating like a student fervently studying for an all-important exam. It was just one more thing that Xan loved about him.

"Hey, Michael."

"Hm?"

"How come you've never asked why I decided not to be turned?"

Michael slowly lowered his comic. The crease in his brow deepened. "Because it's none of my business."

"You're my boyfriend," Xan pointed out. "You have a right to ask."

"No, I don't."

"Sure you do. Don't you ever wonder how things will be... you know... down the road?"

"Yeah, but I try not to think about it." Michael regarded Xan for a bit. "Have *you* been thinking about it?"

"Yeah."

"Since when?"

"Since last night." Xan didn't feel like going into the whole story with Denny just yet, so he skipped forward to the ending. "All this time, I thought it was selfish of me to be turned after being lucky enough to have the life I have. But maybe it's selfish of me not to do it. I don't want to hurt anybody."

Michael placed his comic book on the floor and stretched out his arms. One hand rested on top of Aggie's head and the other on Xan's shin. "I know a thing or two about making choices based on what other people want. Your dads knew what would happen when they adopted you. And I knew it when you told me you wanted to be with me, even though I tried to forget about it. Dominic and Jacob wouldn't want you to do something you're not sure you want to do just to make them happy. I don't want that, either."

"Will you still love me when I'm old and grey?"

"Yes. And will you still love me when you're old and grey and everyone thinks you're a pervert with an Asian kink for being with me?"

"Damn." Xan was horrified at the thought of others equating him with the gross old geezer who had latched onto Michael the night they met. "People are totally going to think that, aren't they?"

"Probably."

"I guess there's no way around it," Xan said, shrugging. "Yes, I'll still love you."

He wasn't sure why Michael gasped at his reply. Eventually, he understood. Xan hadn't been the only one who was unsure of his feelings for Michael.

"I'm sorry I didn't say it sooner. I think I felt it way before I knew it, if that helps."

"It does." Michael smiled sweetly at him. "Let's go to bed."

After coaxing Aggie to the floor, they untangled their legs and stacked all the comics to finish reading later. Xan got up and went to the door to make sure it was locked. On a whim, he opened it instead.

"You've got to be shitting me."

"What is it?" Michael came over and peered around him. "Oh."

Tiny white flakes danced in the wind. While it was cold out, the temperature wasn't low enough for the snow to stick to the ground. Xan was extra glad that he was able to ride his motorcycle one last time. The way things were looking, he wasn't going to have another chance until sometime next year.

"It's not so bad," Michael said, wrapping his arms around Xan's waist.

"The worst is yet to come."

Indeed it was. And it had nothing to do with snow.

Michael pulled Xan back and kicked the door closed, shutting out the cold and the snow and the last remaining traces of darkness.

LIKE FATHERS, LIKE SON

Copyright 2016 by C.L. Ingro
Author's Note: A Harborview Immortals extra. Xan reacts badly when his fathers tell him no, a word he doesn't hear from them very often.

July 2008

XAN WASN'T SURE IF the pink spot on his left cheek was the result of an impending zit, or due to his repeated poking and prodding in search of any blemish on his otherwise flawless skin. Either way, he decided that it was best to leave it alone for now and check back later to see if anything developed. If so, he would take the necessary steps to vanquish the unwanted intruder, using various washes and creams designed for such a purpose or, in a pinch, using a dab of vampire blood. The latter was only in case of an emergency, and getting a zit on the night before the biggest party of the year definitely qualified as one.

He turned away from the mirror and exited the bathroom. Then, after accidentally stepping on the sharp edge of a black Lego piece and cursing a blue streak, he plopped down on his old but comfortable bean bag chair. It was normally the spot where he would read comics and manga or play video games, both for hours on end, but tonight he was too excited to do either.

For someone who had never once stepped foot inside any of Harborview's five high schools, Xan Dawson was becoming quite the guy to know among the older teens of the city. Then again, with his outgoing personality—a rarity for one who had been homeschooled his entire life—and stunning good looks that were courtesy of a biological mother and father he would never know, it was little wonder that everyone wanted a piece of him. Literally, when it came to Ryan Douglas, the seventeen-year-old athletic and academic superstar of Harborview High who was, to borrow one of Becky's phrases, sex on legs. He also happened to be the reason for Xan's present excitement.

They met last month, two weeks after Xan's sixteenth birthday, in the gaming area of the city's largest theater. Xan was at the skee-ball machine as usual; it was a game he had grown remarkably gifted at playing over the many years that his daytime guardian, Luca, escorted him to the movies while his fathers slept. Ryan was playing right beside him, and what started as a mutual respect for the other's skill quickly turned into a competition that attracted the attention of all the other teens in the area who had been looking for ways to waste their money and time before the start of whatever movie they were there to see. Xan won by a scant twenty points, and after using all of his tickets to get a cheap plastic trophy that wasn't worth nearly the amount of money he had spent, he decided to pass up drooling over James McAvoy in *Wanted* to eat greasy slices of pepperoni and sausage pizza while getting to know his new friend.

And so began his journey into local high school society. Everyone wanted to know more about the charming and mysterious kid who had never graced the school halls with his presence. The fact that Ryan had taken an interest in him only further fueled their fascination. Before Xan knew it, he was being invited to all the places around Harborview where most of the kids spent their summer vacations in lieu of staying home. The mall, the bowling alley, the ice skating rink, even the zoo. His new Facebook account—something he was finally allowed to have now that he was sixteen—was constantly bombarded with followers and friend requests, and he got so many text messages on a daily basis that he was contemplating changing his phone number.

However, Xan didn't care about any of that. All he cared about was hanging out with Ryan, who was just as much of a geek as Xan underneath the brains and the brawn. Having only ever spent his life around vampires and Luca, Xan was thrilled to have met someone close to his own age who shared a number of his hobbies.

Two nights ago, when a fierce round of *Mario Kart* led to some playful teenaged frolicking all over Ryan's bedroom floor, which then led to some not-so-playful making out, Xan realized that there were other benefits to this new friendship that he was eager to explore. Benefits that might have been explored at the time if not for a little sister who picked that exact moment to barge in and demand that they attend a tea party alongside esteemed stuffed toy guests.

Benefits that Xan had every intention of exploring tomorrow night at the much-anticipated summer bash for Harborview's upperclassmen.

Despite his newfound popularity, he hadn't expected to be invited to the exclusive gathering because he didn't attend any of the schools in the area. But when Ryan extended the offer with a promising look in his dark brown eyes, Xan knew that he had to go. And so he would... if he was able to overcome the only possible obstacle in his way:

He had to get permission from his parents.

Surely they would say yes. They almost always said yes to whatever Xan wanted. And as long as he was honest—without being *too* honest—about the types of things one might expect to find at a party attended by a bunch of high schoolers with raging hormones, then they would most likely say yes to this, too.

After half an hour spent staring into space and imagining all the things that two guys could do together—then cringing in disgust when he remembered that his dads were also two guys—he decided to go ahead and get the asking done. With that out of the way, he would be free to spend the next twenty-four hours wallowing in anticipation. He got up and stepped into the hallway, where the smell of simmering spaghetti sauce hit his nose and made his stomach growl. One of his favorite things about Fridays were the lavish Italian meals that Dominic prepared for him; Xan felt lucky (and occasionally amused) to have a vampire father with such incredible skill in the kitchen.

He found both his fathers in the office, their heads almost touching as they leaned in close to each other and read over the single sheet of paper between them upon which, Xan presumed, were figures pertaining to one of their two businesses. There was the homeless shelter that was named after Xan, the Dawson House, and their nightclub, the Rising Sun, where Xan planned to work one day. He hadn't yet broke that bit of news to his folks and doubted it would go over well, seeing as how it was a vampires-only establishment. But much like the legion of tattoos he was going to get once he turned eighteen, he knew what he wanted and was fairly positive that he would be able to get it without too much complaint.

"Knock, knock," he said, lightly tapping on the doorway. He almost hated to bother them because while the thought of them having sex made his insides shrivel and rot, seeing them together like this always gave him a warm and fuzzy feeling.

"Hey there." Jacob smiled and waved him in. "I assumed that you would have your nose in one of your anime books until dinner."

Xan groaned and entered the room. "Why do you call them that? You know it drives me crazy."

"Because I know it drives you crazy."

"Thanks, Dad." Grinning, Xan took a seat in an empty chair in front of the desk. "Speaking of dinner, how much longer will it be? I'm starving."

"About twenty minutes," Dominic replied. "Do you think you can make it that long?"

"I'll try." Drumming his fingers on the arms of the chair, Xan took a deep breath and continued as casually as he could, "So... I was wondering if it was okay if I went to a party tomorrow night."

"What kind of party?" Jacob asked. "Will it be chaperoned?"

Xan mulled over how much he wanted to reveal. He decided that broad strokes were the best way to go. "It's a yearly thing that the high school kids do. To celebrate summer and all of that. And I don't think there will be a chaperone but most of the people going are eighteen."

"Where is this party taking place?" Dominic asked.

"The Lamonte Hotel."

When Xan saw them exchange glances, he had a feeling that he was somehow screwed, though not in the way he wanted to be come tomorrow night.

"You mean the Summer Fuck Fling," Jacob said, sitting back in his chair.

"Wh-What?" Xan sputtered. Not because of the party's unofficial nickname, which was well-known among the young adults who attended, but because Jacob also knew about it.

"We've had a professional relationship with the owners of that hotel for years," Dominic explained. "We are well-informed about everything that happens there, including these annual high school events and the illicit activities that take place during them."

"The sex, the alcohol, the drugs..." Jacob shook his head. "I don't suppose you were aware of any of that?"

Xan debated feigning ignorance but opted against it. One of the disadvantages to having vampires as parents was that their senses were sharp enough to immediately detect any minor change in his movements, his breathing, even his heartbeat. They would have known in an instant if he was lying.

"I heard some rumors," he admitted.

"Did you hear the one about the kid who almost overdosed last year?" Jacob asked.

"No." Xan actually hadn't heard about that but he was hardly surprised considering some of the stories he had been told. "I don't plan to do any drinking or drugs myself. That's got to count for something."

He purposely left off the sex part and could tell by the vampires' expressions that doing so had not gone unnoticed.

"Alexander..." Dominic began.

Feeling a rejection coming, Xan immediately interrupted with a last-ditch effort to plead his case. "I promise I won't do anything stupid. Don't you trust me?"

"Yes, we trust you," Dominic replied. "That doesn't mean we trust the ones you'll be with. That kind of environment is hardly appropriate for you."

Jacob nodded in agreement. "Besides, you just turned sixteen. You will have plenty of opportunities to attend plenty of parties in the future."

Xan sighed loudly. This was not at all how he had hoped the conversation would go.

"I don't want to go to plenty of parties. I want to go to *this* one."

"We can't let you do that, Alexander," Dominic responded.

"You understand, don't you?" Jacob asked.

But Xan didn't want to understand. He wanted to hook up with Ryan and do all of the things that he had fantasized about, and he didn't want anyone, not even his dads, to get in the way of that.

He could feel irrational anger bubbling to the surface, steamrolling over the small voice of reason within him that knew damn well that Dominic and Jacob had every reason to refuse his request. It wasn't just about being told no, a word he almost never heard from them. As far as Xan was concerned, this party was going to be his best chance to have some alone time with Ryan without little sisters ruining the fun. With his parents' denial, that chance was slipping right through his fingers. And it pissed him off.

"This is so much bullshit," he snapped, folding his arms and scowling at the vampires. Their lack of reaction over his use of profanity only agitated him further.

"How so?" Dominic asked calmly.

"You're holding things that other people have done or might do against me." Xan stared defiantly at the duo, feeling justified in his explanation. "I don't think that's fair."

"I'm sorry you feel that way, but that doesn't change our answer," Jacob stated. "You're not going."

In a fit of fury, Xan got up and stormed over to the open door. Then, as if it would have made a difference, he spun around and said, "I could have snuck out or lied to you about where I was going."

"You could have, but you're smarter than that," Dominic told him.

"Xan." Jacob scooted forward in his chair, his arms resting on top of the desk. "I know you think that this is a grave injustice, but once you've calmed down, you'll see that we're only doing what's best for you. That's what fathers are supposed to do."

"You're not my fucking fathers!"

Xan had wanted a reaction from them, and with those words, he got one. Dominic stared at him with a slightly raised brow that, for one so sparingly expressive, was akin to open astonishment. That was bad enough. But it was the look of shock and dismay and *hurt* on Jacob's face that did Xan in. Whatever measure of triumph he thought that getting a rise out of them would give him was immediately negated by a sense of regret unlike anything he had ever felt before.

Suddenly, going to a party seemed like the most insignificant thing in the world.

"I... I didn't mean to say that."

Dominic stood up. "I need to check the sauce."

He rounded the desk and left the office without saying another word.

Xan stared at the vampire's retreating back until he could no longer see him and then turned to face Jacob. "Dad—"

"You should help Luca set the table," Jacob said quietly.

The teen stood his ground, not wanting to leave but also knowing that no good could come from staying. Neither vampire wanted to talk to him right now, and he could hardly blame them. With an ache in his heart and the sting of tears in his eyes, he slowly made his way into the dining room where Luca was waiting for him with a handful of silverware and a sympathetic look.

"You heard?"

"Not all of it," the big man answered. "Just the worst of it."

Xan lowered his head. He was starting to feel physically ill from the shame and revulsion over his childish behavior.

"I'm an asshole, Luca," he mumbled. It was not an attempt to solicit pity, but a genuine assessment of his character as he—and Dominic and Jacob, undoubtedly—saw it.

"You're a teenager," Luca countered. "Being an asshole comes with the territory every now and then." When the doorbell sounded, he handed the silverware over to Xan and ruffled his stylishly messy blond hair. "Now chin up. We've got company."

Xan finished setting the table while Luca left to answer the door. He found some comfort in knowing that the older man would never judge him. It was one of the reasons he still had a crush on him, a lifelong secret he planned to take to the grave.

He was hardly in the mood to be social, but he also didn't want to make a terrible situation even worse. Therefore, he gave his best imitation of a smile when Becky and Demetrio entered the dining room and took turns smothering him with hugs and kisses.

"How's my little Xanadu tonight?" Becky asked as she took a seat at the table.

"I'm good." Xan saw by the tilt of her head that she didn't believe him but was thankfully spared further interrogation when Jacob arrived to greet their guests. He sat down next to Becky while Demetrio launched into a highly explicit account of his latest conquest involving another vampire, a bottle of lube, and some very large anal beads.

Jacob rolled his eyes as he poured red wine for the adults and water for Xan. "Come on, Demetrio. Not in front of my kid."

The statement gave Xan hope. If Jacob was still willing to refer to him as his kid then maybe he didn't completely hate him after all.

Demetrio winked at his nephew. "I'm sure he won't be scarred for life by a little anal bead talk."

"You better not let Dominic hear you talking like that," Jacob warned him.

"Too late." Dominic stood in the dining room doorway with a large serving bowl filled to the brim with spaghetti and meatballs. He glared at his twin brother—his standard way of greeting him. "If you would be so kind as to refrain from sharing tales of your whoredom, it would be greatly appreciated."

"I'm not a whore, Domenico," Demetrio insisted. "I prefer to think of myself as a sexual connoisseur."

Becky snorted into her wine glass while Jacob held a hand to his mouth to hide his grin. Even Xan couldn't help but crack a hint of a smile at his uncle's ridiculousness.

As Demetrio and Luca followed Dominic into the kitchen to help with the rest of the food, the teen risked a glance at Jacob, who was now conversing with Becky. There were no signs of the emotional devastation that Xan had witnessed not even ten minutes ago. Was he imagining what he thought he saw back in the office? Had he overestimated the effect his verbal eruption had on Jacob?

No, that wasn't it. While it would have been easier to believe that his words had rolled off the vampire like water, the truth was that Jacob was simply being a good host. The Friday family dinners were a big to-do in their house, and had been for quite some time. Of course Jacob would see to it that the occasion wasn't ruined because of Xan's tantrum.

Once everything was in order and everyone was seated around the table, Xan and Luca dug in as the vampires contented themselves with blood. Xan no longer had much of an appetite, but he managed to eat just enough not to draw attention to himself while the others chatted about current events and politics. The hot topic of the night was some biracial Senator from Illinois who stood a good chance at becoming President. Jacob, being biracial himself, was especially interested in him and expressed his disappointment that vampires were unable to vote.

After the meal was finished, Xan remained at the table for what he considered to be an acceptable amount of time before excusing himself to escape to his bedroom. He dutifully said his goodbyes and ran upstairs, then went into his room and—after stepping on that damned Lego piece once again—fell facedown on the bed. He didn't even bother checking his phone for missed calls and messages, which was usually the first thing he did after dinner since cell phones were not allowed at the table. Now that he was alone and no longer had the burden of putting up a brave front, he replayed those appalling words in his head over and over until he was certain that he was going to cry or throw up or, most likely, both.

About twenty minutes later, Xan felt someone watching him from the doorway. He knew who it was even before the soothing sound of an English accent hit his ears.

"What did you do?"

Xan turned to regard Becky and felt like even more of a jerk. He much preferred her playful insults and endless teasing to the worried countenance he saw now. "I fucked up."

"How?" She crossed the room and, after nudging his legs out of the way, sat down on the edge of the bed. "Tell me."

There was no way around it. Xan closed his eyes and swallowed hard. Then he told her everything.

"Xan!" Becky exclaimed in horror when he was finished. "I ought to smack you silly. It would hardly be the first time, but this time you would deserve it."

Xan buried his face again. "I know," he muttered into his pillow.

"Short of calling Jacob the N-word, that is the *worst thing* you could have ever said to either of them."

Upon hearing Becky liken what he had said to something he would have never said, no matter how upset he was, the dam finally broke and the tears came forth. He thought about all of the things his parents had ever done for him, how he wouldn't even be alive if not for them, and sobbed even harder into the pillow. Nothing, not even the hand that was now gently stroking his back, could ease the pain he felt over having acted like such a spoiled and ungrateful shit.

"What will you do now?" Becky asked as she pulled him up and hugged him tightly. "Sit up here and mope for the rest of the night?"

That was precisely what Xan had planned to do because he wasn't sure if Dominic or Jacob even wanted to look at him, let alone talk to him.

"Come on, love." She rose from the bed and helped him to his feet. After taking a handkerchief out of her bra—she didn't carry a purse—she wiped his tears away, her expression stern but loving. "Now you need to go set things right. Like I always say, never let the sun rise on an argument."

"You don't say that."

"Well, I'm saying it now. Here, clean your nose. You're getting snot all over the place."

Xan took the offered handkerchief and blew his nose. Afterwards, he shoved the soiled cloth back down the vampire's low-cut top because he still had an obligation to annoy her.

"Oh, that's just gross. You're lucky I love you." Becky removed the handkerchief and tossed it on top of Xan's bed. After a moment, she thoughtfully added, "They love you, too. No matter what asinine things you say."

Xan nodded and ducked his head. A slender finger slid beneath his chin and lifted it back up.

"Never say that again." Becky's tone was polite, but also dead serious.

"I won't." Xan couldn't promise not to say stupid things from time to time, but as for implying that the two vampires who had taken him in weren't his fathers? Never again.

They went downstairs. Luca and Demetrio were gone. Dominic and Jacob were nowhere to be found, but Xan had a good idea where they were. After Becky punched him on the arm for luck and left, he went to the door that led out to the rear deck. He couldn't see them yet from where he stood, but he knew that they were there.

Xan took a minute to compose himself before moving on. As he drew closer to the seats that were positioned to look out on Lake Erie, he saw the couple sitting on the patio sofa. He stopped a few feet away from them, his hands curled into fists at his side and his heart racing.

"Your heart sounds like it is about to burst out of your chest," Dominic said, breaking the silence. "Just like that grotesque alien movie you enjoy so much. What is it called?"

"*Aliens*," Jacob answered.

"*Aliens?*" Dominic was unimpressed. "That isn't very original."

"It gets the point across."

Xan didn't know how to process the two of them nonchalantly discussing one of his favorite movies while he was standing there in the midst of his inner turmoil. Weren't they angry with him?

He spoke up before he lost what little courage he had mustered. "Um... can I talk to you guys for a second? Please?"

"Of course," Dominic replied.

Xan tried not to fidget as they watched him expectantly, waiting for him to continue. "I just wanted to say that I'm really sorry for the way I acted before dinner," he started, studying his bare feet. "And for what I said about the two of you... not being my fathers. I didn't mean it. I would give anything to take it back."

His voice had started to waver by the time he got to the last sentence, and he bit his quivering lip in an attempt to stave off a fresh round of tears. Frowning, he steeled himself for whatever might happen next, be it a firm lecture or scolding or whatever unpleasantness would surely ensue.

"We know you're sorry," Jacob began.

"And we forgive you," Dominic concluded.

Xan raised his head and gawked at them. "... You're not mad at me?"

To the teen's complete amazement, Jacob chuckled. "You almost sound disappointed."

"No, but... I don't know. Don't you want to yell at me or ground me or something?"

"I don't see any reason for that," Dominic said. "Besides, I suspect that you're punishing yourself more than we ever could."

That was certainly true. They were apparently willing to forgive him without so much as a harsh word, but Xan knew that it was going to be a while before he forgave himself for the way he had behaved.

Jacob scooted over and patted the empty cushion between him and Dominic. Normally, Xan would have balked at joining them because it made him feel like the kid he no longer wanted to be, but he resigned himself to making an exception for tonight. It was the least he could do.

He sat down between them with a drawn-out sigh of relief masquerading as inconvenience. When arms wrapped around him from both sides, he was too delighted to pretend that he hated it.

"It *did* sting a little, the way you lashed out at us," Jacob admitted. He reached out with his free hand and tugged on one of the four platinum hoops in Xan's right ear. "But we weren't mad. We just needed some time to absorb it."

"Who is the young gentleman?" Dominic asked. "He must be quite the individual to inspire such an outburst."

Xan grinned. He wasn't surprised that they had figured it out. "Ryan Douglas."

"The nerdy jock?" Jacob inquired.

"Yeah."

"Is he your boyfriend?" Dominic wanted to know.

"No, we're just friends," Xan replied with a firm shake of the head. "I don't want to go out with him. I just want..."

"Sex?" Jacob suggested.

"Ew, Dad!"

"Ew, what? Sex is a perfectly natural thing to want. I want it constantly."

"Yes, he does," Dominic agreed.

Xan shuddered and let loose a series of gagging noises. "I thought you guys weren't going to punish me."

With an evil snicker, Jacob squeezed his son's shoulder. "Not that I want to think about it, but you will have plenty of opportunities for *that* in the future, too."

Xan craned his neck and stared at the crescent moon high above them. It awed him to know that it was the same moon that had shone down on Dominic and Jacob so many centuries ago.

He still wanted Ryan, and if all went well, he would have him. Not tomorrow night, as it turned out. But eventually.

"I guess," he conceded, putting the matter to rest for now. "So can I hang out here with the two of you, or do you want me to go inside so you can get back to whatever you were doing? What were you doing, anyway?"

"We were discussing which one of us is responsible for your stubbornness." Jacob cast an accusatory glance at his partner. "Dominic thinks it's my fault."

"Because it is," Dominic said.

"What about you?"

"I'm not stubborn."

Both Jacob and Xan laughed at that.

"I hate to burst your bubble, Domi, but you *are* pretty stubborn." Xan twirled a lock of the vampire's long black hair around his fingers—something he hadn't done since he was a child—and jerked his head toward Jacob. "You just hide it better than this one."

"He is rather theatrical at times, isn't he?"

"He sure is."

Jacob cleared his throat. Theatrically. "I'm right here, you know."

Xan smiled as they continued their debate. After adamantly stating their respective opinions, they turned to him for a final answer.

"I think I get it from both of you equally," he decided. "Like fathers, like son."

"That works for me," Jacob said after thinking it over.

"I guess I don't mind sharing the blame," Dominic added, nodding.

Xan kissed them both on the cheek. "Good."

He looked ahead, admiring the tranquility of the lake. His eyes were stinging again, although the tears that threatened this time were happy ones. Xan was thankful that his foolishness resulted in what he would one day look back on as one of the most perfect moments of his charmed life, sitting there snug between the two vampires. His parents. His fathers.

Because they *were* his fathers. Maybe not by blood, but in every other way that mattered.

LAST SUMMER

Copyright 2016 by C.L. Ingro
Author's Note: A Harborview Immortals extra. It's summertime and Xan plans to spend most of it creating memories with a very special friend.

July 2009

IT NEVER FAILED TO amuse Xan when people referred to the public miles-long stretch of Harborview shore along the edge of Lake Erie as the beach. While he supposed that the word was technically correct, it was hardly what he had in mind when he thought about beaches. Beaches went hand in hand with oceans. Actual oceans, like the Pacific or Atlantic. Lake Erie, while vast in its own right, was not an ocean. It wasn't even the greatest of all the Great Lakes. It was, however, the best he could hope for living in Northwest Pennsylvania short of trekking to the East Coast to see what he considered to be the real thing.

He spread an oversized towel on the sand and sat down, his long legs stretching out across the thick green material. The heat from the midday sun was slightly offset by a gentle breeze, and he closed his eyes and craned his neck toward the sky to savor both. He felt a stab of guilt for being able to enjoy the sunshine while his fathers were presently stuck in the house, confined to the basement until sundown. Although there were obvious advantages to being a vampire, like immortality, it was during moments like these when Xan could fully appreciate being a mere human who could bask in the rays without melting into a puddle of bloody goo.

After a few minutes of soaking up the sun—and hoping that he had applied enough sunblock to ward off any burning—he opened his eyes and stared out at the lake. Luca had once told him that you could see clear across to Canada if the conditions were just right, but all he could see right now was water, deep blue and seemingly endless. Four or five jet skis raced across his line of sight and there were a number of boats farther out that looked like little white specks against a blue backdrop. People frolicked in the water here and there, scattered about, but the view that interested Xan the most was closer to land. And what a view it was.

"See something you like?" Ryan asked as he exited the lake.

Xan smiled as the teen shook the excess water off his muscular arms and legs before joining him. "Maybe," he said, handing him a spare towel.

"It's nothing you haven't seen before." Ryan blotted his face with the towel and placed it on the ground beside Xan. "Up close and personal," he added with a smirk while taking a seat.

"Yeah, but it's going to be a while before I see it again."

"I'm only going to New York, and it's not like I'm never coming back. Besides, absence makes the heart grow fonder and all that crap."

That was all well and good, but it wasn't Xan's heart that was going to miss Ryan.

They met one year ago at the movies and quickly bonded over skee-ball and pizza. It was the first time that Xan ever had a friend close to his own age, human or otherwise. Shortly afterwards, they discovered that their mutual interests extended to each other. While neither teen was looking for a boyfriend for their own respective reasons—Ryan just wanted to focus on school and Xan just wanted to focus on getting off—they managed to find the perfect balance between friendship and physical enjoyment. Now that Ryan was leaving for college in a few weeks, Xan was lamenting the inevitable end to a rather pleasurable aspect of their non-relationship.

"We'll talk on the phone and online, just like we do now," Ryan continued. "Nothing's going to change... except for that one thing."

"I like that one thing," Xan said.

"Me too."

Ryan reached across Xan and grabbed a bottle of water from the cooler lodged in the sand. Xan studied the light sprinkle of freckles across his well-tanned arm and shoulder and resisted the urge to trace them as he had done so many times before when they were alone.

"Are we hanging out tonight?" Ryan asked after taking a drink.

"I thought you were going to the Summer Fuck Fling. It's your last chance to go."

Ryan shrugged. "I did enough partying the week of graduation. I'm partied out. Unless you want to go?"

Xan thought back to the year before, when his parents' refusal to let him attend the upperclassmen party of the year resulted in some unfortunate behavior on his part. Now that he was seventeen, he had no reason to believe that they would deny him the opportunity, but the thought held little appeal if Ryan didn't want to go.

"It doesn't matter to me," he answered. "Whatever you want to do."

"My parents and sister are home so we can't do what I *really* want to do. But I finally got the new *Resident Evil* game so at least there's that."

"That sounds like a lot more fun than getting drunk and possibly laid," Xan replied sarcastically. "'Yay.'"

He didn't bother trying to dodge the playful punch that landed on his upper arm, and was glad that he didn't when Ryan's hand lingered, then opened, then cupped his bicep. A thumb started stroking his skin, sending a jolt down his arm.

"People can see us," he warned.

"Do you care?"

"No, but maybe you should. You're Harborview's golden boy, after all."

"Don't remind me," Ryan muttered, pulling away from him and taking another drink of water. "That's the biggest reason I can't wait to get the hell out of here. I'm tired of people expecting greatness from me."

"Can you blame them? You're an honor student and varsity letterman in pretty much every sport ever. You're like the poster child for overachievement." Xan shifted to the right and nudged the teen in the side. "There are way worse things in life than being good at everything you do, Ryan."

"I know, but it's still annoying." Ryan finished off his water and let out a respectable belch. He leaned back on his hands and stretched his legs alongside Xan's. "Anyway, you don't want to lose your virginity at some party with a bunch of drunk assholes in the next room, do you?"

Had Xan been asked that question a year ago, his answer would have been a resounding yes. He had wanted it so badly that he lashed out and insulted his fathers, an act that still made him feel awful twelve months later. But now?

"I guess not," he replied. "I mean, I don't need candlelight and love songs and shit, but no, I don't want some idiots who can't handle their liquor puking their guts out one room over, either."

"And I imagine you don't want to do it on my poor excuse for a bed."

"Why not? We've done just about everything else on it."

"True," Ryan responded, chuckling. "But do you honestly want your first time to be a race against the clock in case someone comes home? I don't." He turned toward Xan and leaned forward. "I'm going to need a whole night for all the things I want to do to you."

Xan shuddered as a tongue ran along the five platinum hoops in his ear. If Ryan insisted on teasing him like this, the question of when and where they were going to do it wasn't going to be an issue because he was going to jump on him right then and there, onlookers be damned.

"Come on," Ryan said suddenly, slapping him on the back. "Let's swim."

"I'm going to need a minute."

The older teen laughed. "It'll go down once you're in the water," he said as he stood up and held out his hand. "Let's go."

Xan reluctantly took Ryan's hand and allowed the young man to pull him to his feet. With a kind smile and a knowing look in his dark brown eyes, Ryan squeezed Xan's hand briefly before letting go, a silent gesture that perfectly summed up the friendship that was and the relationship that would never be.

They raced each other into the water—Ryan won easily—and spent the next half hour swimming and splashing about. Somewhere along the way, Xan realized that he was wrong in his earlier assessment. Quite wrong.

He was going to miss this, too.

AN HOUR LATER, AFTER rinsing off in the beach's pitiful excuse for a shower and getting dressed, the boys stopped at the nearest Dairy King for a late lunch. They hurriedly worked their way through cheeseburgers and fries before digging into two large sundaes that were more hot fudge than ice cream.

Two young women from Ryan's high school attempted to join them, but Ryan immediately, though politely, denied their efforts.

"Heartbreaker," Xan accused while chomping on a maraschino cherry.

"Better heartbreaker than cockblocker," Ryan shot back. Xan couldn't disagree.

After that, they went to the theater and watched *Harry Potter and the Half-Blood Prince*. Xan didn't remember much about the movie, but he distinctly remembered the way that Ryan's hand felt on his thigh for two and a half hours.

When the movie ended, they entertained themselves by heading for the gaming area and revisiting their skee-ball rivalry. Xan bested Ryan more often than not, and he blew all of his hard-earned tickets on a variety of small stuffed animals that he planned to give to Ryan's little sister in the hopes that she would keep her distance later that evening.

Next, they went to Booksen More, one of the last locally owned bookstores in the city. (Xan had no idea that the owner was the son of the man who once owned an adult store named Coxen Things, which was where his parents were headed the night they found him.) They did their part to ensure the economic survival of the store by dropping a massive amount of money on comic books and manga. From there, they swung by the mall but left soon after when it became apparent that their presence would not go unnoticed by other teens.

By the time evening rolled around, they were hungry again, so they picked up a pizza and went back to Ryan's house. The stuffed animal bribe was a success, although Xan had to sweeten the deal with a slice of pizza as well. They ate and read comics and debated topics of vital importance such as whether or not Iron Man was better than Batman. Ryan was a staunch supporter of Bruce Wayne while Xan was firmly Team Tony Stark, though they both agreed that Superman was the best of all... until Xan boldly announced that Goku could beat Superman and prompted a new argument about hypothetical fights between manga and comic book characters.

After they finished eating, they settled on the floor of Ryan's bedroom for some *Resident Evil 5*. They played well into the night, stopping only for bathroom breaks and so that Xan could text Jacob to let him know he was still alive and behaving himself. Ryan had shut off his own phone an hour earlier to silence the texts and calls requesting his presence at the Summer Fuck Fling.

"What time am I taking you home?" he asked when they resumed gaming.

Xan waited until they destroyed a particularly difficult zombie before replying. "Whenever you want. Oh yeah, remind me to give you gas money."

"Keep it. You can put it toward buying your own car."

"I have my own car. Dominic just hasn't given it to me yet."

"You seem pretty sure that he will."

"He's had the damn thing for thirty years. It's time for an upgrade." Xan cursed when an attack nearly drained his character's health. "I think he's going to make me wait until I'm eighteen."

Ryan cringed, though it was hard to say if it was because of Xan's comment or nearly having his ass handed to him by a zombie. "That sucks." (This also applied to both instances.)

When they had their fill of fighting the undead, they switched off the game. While Ryan crept into the kitchen to grab a couple of Cokes, Xan wandered around the room and marveled at the many displays of his friend's achievements. It was nothing he hadn't seen before, but he also knew that he wouldn't have many more chances to do this again after Ryan moved out. Trophies and medals and certificates were everywhere he turned, all of them highlighting Ryan's success in sports and education. Xan paused at a dresser to study framed pictures of the teen posing in football, baseball, and track attire, plus another one from the senior prom of him and three friends looking mighty fine in their tuxedos. The newest photo in the collection was of Ryan in his black cap and gown, smiling cheerfully as a blue and black tassel dangled in his face, the very same tassel that now hung from the rearview mirror in his car as a constant reminder of his graduation. Xan thought he looked especially handsome in this picture, and he was so busy staring at it that he didn't notice when Ryan entered the room and came up behind him.

"Here you go." He handed Xan a cold can of Coke and peered over his shoulder. "Do you ever regret being homeschooled?"

Although there were a few occasions over the years when Xan had wondered what it was like to sit in an actual classroom while being taught by an actual teacher as opposed to sitting at home and being taught by Luca, he never felt that he was lacking socially so much that he needed to attend one of Harborview's many high schools. There was also the matter of privacy. He was the unofficial adoptee of two centuries-old vampires. Going to a public school would have undoubtedly invited questions about his identity that were best left unanswered. He already had enough difficulty keeping that side of his life from Ryan. Thankfully, the young man was smart enough to sense that there were certain truths that Xan was never going to divulge about his family and never pressed the subject.

"No. It's one thing to see other kids whenever I'm out. I don't know how I'd like being stuck in a classroom with them every day."

"It's not always fun." Ryan cracked open his soda and took a long drink. "Have you decided what you're going to do after you're done?"

"College, I guess. I'll probably do most of it online, or take a few classes at Mercymore or Penn State. I'm not exactly sure yet."

"What do you want to study?"

Xan shrugged as he returned the picture to its rightful place and opened his drink. "I have no idea."

He neglected to add that he didn't care because his ultimate goal was bartending in his fathers' vampires-only nightclub, the Rising Sun. Like the tattoos that had fascinated him since he was thirteen, it was something Xan had wanted for a long time. While a degree was hardly necessary for the job, he also knew that Dominic and Jacob would have had a combined fit if he had announced that he was skipping college entirely. It was going to be hard enough to talk them into letting him work at the club; if nothing else, at least this way he would have four years to convince them.

"You'll figure it out," Ryan assured him. "And definitely take some classes in person if you can. The scenery will be a lot nicer."

"That is a good reason," Xan acknowledged. He downed a bit of the fizzy beverage and pressed the back of his hand to his mouth to stifle a burp. "You're going to be hooking up with so many hot guys. I'm jealous."

"Of them?"

"Of *you.*"

Ryan grinned and placed his free hand on Xan's waist. "I'll be sure to give you all the dirty details," he promised.

"Damn right, you will."

Xan spun around and blinked at his friend, pleasantly aware of how close he was standing. He grabbed onto Ryan's shirt and pulled him even closer, reducing the space between them until their lips collided and tongues intertwined. The older teen pushed Xan back and trapped him between the dresser and his body, and Xan moaned into a mouth that tasted like soda and pepperoni and a hint of mint, one hand clinging to Ryan's shirt and the other crushing his Coke can.

Eventually he broke the kiss, while he still possessed the ability to do so. "Shit," he whispered, his chest heaving and his limbs shaking. "You should probably take me home now."

"Yeah," Ryan agreed breathlessly. He glanced down at his shirt. "I will as soon as you let go of me."

Xan pried his fingers loose and handed him the dented can. He collected his things and followed Ryan through the dark house and out to his car.

Conversation reverted to their usual geekish discussions as Ryan drove him home, like the upcoming *G.I. Joe* movie and whether or not there was any truth to the rumors they had read online about a television adaptation of *The Walking Dead* comic book. By the time Ryan turned onto Shore Harbor Drive, Xan had more or less recovered from their moment against the dresser, although he had a feeling that the experience spawned an itch that would need to be scratched before he went to sleep.

"What are you doing next weekend?" Ryan asked after pulling into the driveway of Xan's house.

"I assumed I was hanging out with you, unless you have other plans."

"Do you want to spend the night?"

Of course Xan wanted to spend the night. There was only one small problem, the same problem that had prevented him from staying over tonight. "Aren't your parents going to be home?"

"Yeah, but..." Ryan's eyes darted toward the house, perhaps to make sure that no one was spying on them (which was not a far-fetched fear when it came to the fiercely overprotective Jacob). "I was thinking that we could get a room. A hotel room. So... you know... you would still be spending the night with me. Just not at my house."

"Yeah, let's... let's do that." Xan nodded emphatically. "We *really* need to do that."

Ryan chortled at his eagerness. "We do. I'll talk to you later."

"See you."

Xan got out and waved as Ryan backed out of the driveway. He stayed put until he couldn't see the car's taillights anymore and remained a little while longer to wallow in the excitement of what was to come before having to put on a straight face for Dominic and Jacob (one that they would surely see right through because parents were psychic like that). After twelve months of wanting and waiting, it was finally going to happen. Finally! Out of the many memories of his time with Ryan, ones already made and yet to come, Xan knew that he would cherish their first time together most of all. Despite whatever happened afterwards and wherever their lives led them, they would always be bound by that.

He turned and stepped inside with a newfound anticipation that would only grow stronger throughout the upcoming week. His last summer with Ryan was going to be the best summer ever.

Thank you so much for reading this book. For more information about the *Harborview Immortals* series plus other writing projects and random geekery, please visit cl-ingro.com. You may also reach me directly at CLIngro.Author@gmail.com.